Call Me Cass

a Cass Adams novel

Kelly Stone Gamble

Call Me Cass

Red Adept Publishing, LLC

104 Bugenfield Court

Garner, NC 27529

http://RedAdeptPublishing.com/

For Dillon and Theron.

One day, you will have to make decisions for me. Remember I dedicated a book to you. And don't send me to a taxidermist. That was a joke.

Author's note: No Chihuahuas were hurt in the making of this novel.

"Our mothers always remain the strangest, craziest people we've ever met." — Marguerite Duras

Chapter 1
Cass

My feet are swollen, I can barely get out of a chair without doing a backbend, and Peanut kicks me, nonstop, like he's training for the NFL. Or she. I try to reposition myself, but the baby doesn't seem to like the way I move, and he kicks me right in the ribs, which causes me to hiss loud enough to bring Maryanne running from the kitchen.

"Are you okay?" She's wiping her hands on a dish towel, which means she's most likely been doing my dishes. At least there is one good thing about being pregnant.

"Define 'okay,'" I say as I lift my shirt and point at the moving mass that was once my abdomen. Maryanne reaches out to put her hand on my stomach to feel Peanut, and I growl at her. She thinks it's cute, but that's because she doesn't have a tiny human feeding off of her like she's an alien host. And I'm not too happy about everybody thinking that just because I have a baby inside me, they can touch my stomach. I let Clay, because he's Clay, and I let Grams, because she's Grams. But everybody else needs to back off before I strap a bear trap around my waist. It couldn't weigh more than a few pounds, and at this point, I'm sure I wouldn't notice.

I push my phone across the table to Maryanne. "Call Clay again. I need my cheese coney."

"I just called him. I swear. You can wait five more minutes. And besides, you should be eating healthier. Hot dogs can't be good for you."

"Hot dogs smothered in chili, cheese, and onions," I correct her.

She rolls her eyes at me. "Did you take your vitamins today?"

Eat healthier, take your vitamins, do your exercises, get some sleep... The worst thing about being pregnant is having an army of babysitters who won't leave you alone. I know what I need, and it begins with cheese and ends with coney.

"Don't you and Angus have something to do tonight?" I ask her. With all that's been going on with her lately, I'd think Maryanne has better things to do than worry about me. She's getting ready to go back to school for her master's degree in education, and she's been having second thoughts about all the time and work it's going to take to get it. Meanwhile, Angus, her boyfriend, is building a house on Booker Hill, the land he bought from me.

Angus asked Maryanne to move in with him. I hear people talk, between working at the tattoo shop and stopping in Murphy's for my daily piece of lemon meringue pie, and I know a lot of folks in town think the Maryanne-and-Angus thing is crazy. Even though she's a sixth grade teacher, she has a reputation for sleeping with any man who's handy, and it's hard for some people to see how one man, Angus, could possibly be enough for her. She's also a foot taller than him, and when they get all cozy, they look like a swirl cone from the Dairy Queen. Some people, regardless of what they'd like you to believe, are a little bit racist and a whole lot dwarfist. I don't really care what most people think. They'd be better off minding their own business. Besides, I've seen a lot crazier things than Maryanne and Angus. Like the fact that I'm pregnant with my husband's brother's baby. The husband I killed last year. The brother I moved in with.

"He's filling in at the police department tonight," Maryanne says of Angus. "Apparently, with the—"

"I don't care." I hoist myself out of my chair and look out the front window. Dog is following me around like he thinks he's going to get a bite of my cheese coney, if it ever gets here. "And I really don't need a babysitter," I say over my shoulder.

"Oh, stop," she says. "You're within two weeks of your due date, and we just don't want you to be alone, that's all. Be happy you have so many people that care about you. When I was pregnant with Shaylene—"

"I don't care," I say again. I just want my cheese coney and to not have to listen to Maryanne talk about her favorite subject: herself. "When is Shaylene supposed to be here?"

Shaylene is Clay and Maryanne's daughter. Well, really, my husband Roland and Maryanne's daughter, but Clay adopted her when she was a baby so she'd have a good daddy instead of my ass of a husband. Shaylene is off at college, her first year at Kansas University, and she's coming home for the summer break. I can't imagine why an eighteen-year-old girl wouldn't rather be sitting on a beach somewhere and spending her summer break doing Jell-O shots until she pukes, but I'm guessing she wants to join the "keep an eye on the pregnant woman" army. But that's okay, because Shaylene isn't irritating. And she'll fetch me cheese coneys.

"She has a softball tournament tomorrow and said she'll be here by early Tuesday morning. Which means about noon." She lets out a long sigh.

"You haven't told her yet about you and Angus moving in together, have you?" Maryanne and Angus have been dating for a while, and Shaylene likes the guy. So I don't see the big deal about telling Shaylene that they're moving in together this summer. But Maryanne does.

"No, I figure it's better to tell her in person. You know, just in case—"

"Oh, great, there he is!" Clay parks his truck in his usual spot, and I open the door for him and the big bag he's brought from Sonic.

"I got you six, so if you want one in the middle of the night, I can heat it up," he says. "Are you feeling okay?"

I grab the bag from him and stand on my tiptoes to kiss him on the cheek. He's worse than the women hens pecking at me these days. "I'm hungry. Peanut is hungry. And Dog can't find his worm toy."

He scratches Dog on the head, and they go off together in search of Worm. I sit at the table and rip into one of my chili cheese coneys, with extra onions. One bite, and Peanut is doing somersaults. *I know, Peanut. I feel the same way.*

"Have you figured out a name yet?" Maryanne says.

"Peanut works," I say in between bites. Of course, I'm really not going to name my kid Peanut, but she knows I'm a little loony, and I like to see her roll her eyes, thinking I might actually be considering it. No, Peanut would be a stupid name.

She has to know I'm kidding, but she's not biting. The Angus thing must be pretty heavy on her mind. "Seriously, I kind of like Wednesday for a girl," I say.

That gets her attention. "Wednesday Adams? And I suppose Pugsley for a boy." Eye roll.

Gotcha. The truth is, Clay and I haven't figured out a name yet. We talked a little bit about it, but we both figure once we see him, or her, we'll just know. So we're waiting.

"Found it in the nursery." Clay comes back, followed by Dog with his worm toy, and plops into a chair next to me. "How are you feeling?"

I look at him sideways and cram another coney in my mouth. He puts his hands up in front of him, palms out. "Just asking," he says.

Clay is the best thing that's ever happened to me. I've known him since we were kids and from being married to his brother for so many years. But until I moved in with him last summer, I had no idea what a great man he really is. He takes care of me, Dog, and his worm farm, and he'll be the best daddy. He's not perfect; no man is, but he's pretty damn close in my eyes. I'm sure I don't tell him that enough, but he knows how I feel. I haven't killed him, which is more than I can say about his brother.

My phone rings, and I ignore it until it stops. Then Clay's rings, and he answers it on the first ding. "Hello? Yeah, she's doing fine... Great, I'm working tomorrow, and she's insisting on going to the shop, so that will be perfect... Oh, she'll be excited to hear that... I'll let her know that too."

"What am I going to be excited about?" I ask when he hangs up. I know it was Grams. She calls every hour that she isn't here.

"Lola is coming on Friday to stay for a few weeks. You know, to help out," he says.

I groan. I love my sister, but she's a control freak. I guess every army needs a general. Last year, she took in a girl who was pregnant, tried to help her go it alone, but the kid up and ran off with the loser baby daddy about a month ago, and Lola hasn't heard from her since. She's been real sad because I know she really wanted that baby around, but now she'll have Peanut to spoil, so I guess she'll get over it.

"What else did Grams say?" I ask before taking another bite.

Clay starts gathering the empty wrappers off the table then throws them in the trash. "She said to tell you there's a storm coming." He doesn't seem concerned, but I stop chewing and put down my coney.

We live in Kansas, so in springtime and early summer, there's always a storm coming. Grams knows it, and I know it too. So if Grams feels she needs to warn me that one is headed our way, she isn't talking about a little rain. She means it's time to prepare for something epic. A real storm. A big storm.

But I already know about the monster storm headed our way.

Since I've been pregnant, I've been having visions. I guess that's what Grams would call them. At first, I thought my pills were just making me see funny things, but then I realized that what I was seeing was actually things that would happen. For instance, at Christmas, I saw Clay's truck in a ditch, and not five minutes later, he called to tell me he'd slid off the road on the ice. I thought it was just coincidence, but that's not the only thing I've seen. Some things have been good and some not so good, and most of them don't make a lot of sense. But the further along in my pregnancy I get, the more I'm seeing, and the stronger the visions are. A few days ago, I saw Tina Early and Benny Cloud doting over some guy who looked like he'd been spit out of a wood chipper. And this morning, I swear I was standing in the middle of the biggest tornado that's ever come through Deacon, Kansas.

I waddle over to the couch and lie down.

Clay follows and props my feet up on a couch pillow. "What's wrong?"

I know Clay believes in Grams's visions and things. He's seen some of it in the time he's been around, but he's still skeptical, and I don't really want to say anything to him about the storm. Besides, I haven't told him at all about me seeing things, because I'm hoping when the baby is born, it will all go away and I'll just go back to being normal crazy: seeing dead people once in a while instead of seeing things in the future. He doesn't know about the dead-people thing either. With the baby coming soon and Shaylene coming in two days, Clay's got enough on his mind. I don't want him to think I'm any nuttier than he already thinks I am.

"Nothing. Everything's perfect," I say.

Clay puts the rest of my cheese coneys in the refrigerator and takes Dog out to pee.

Maryanne sits next to me in a chair and puts her hand on my arm. "Are you sure you're okay?"

My head starts to swirl, and things go black. Suddenly, I'm standing on a beach. It's so real I can feel the hot, gritty sand between my toes. I shade my eyes and look around and see Maryanne and Roland. She's sitting, and he's standing in front of her, holding his hand out to help her up.

"What?" I say as I'm suddenly back on the couch. I look around quickly, and Maryanne is still next to me, but no Roland. Thank God.

"You blacked out or something. I'm going to get Clay." She starts to get up, but I stop her.

"No, I'm fine. I'm just tired," I say.

She lets out a deep sigh. "I'm your best friend, Cass. If something's wrong, you know you can tell me."

She's right. She is my best friend, one of the only ones I have, and I've told her a lot of things I wouldn't tell anyone else. But I just had a vision of her with my dead husband. And the only way for that to happen would be if she's dead too.

And I don't know how to tell her that.

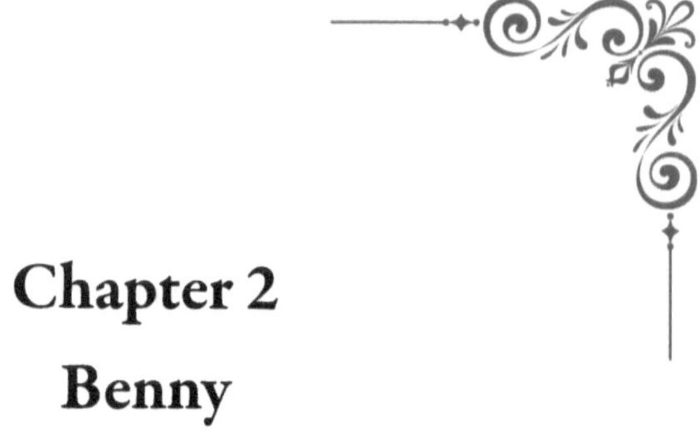

Chapter 2
Benny

After losing the election for sheriff two months ago, I figured I'd be the most pissed off guy in town. After all, it'd been a long time coming, and I'd really wanted to beat Rudy Drown. It was a huge blow to my egotistical ass at the time, but when I think about it now, I'm not sure I really wanted to be sheriff as much as I just wanted Rudy to be cut down to size. And if I were being honest, after all the health problems I've had in the past few months, I don't know that I'd have done the county justice taking on the job of sheriff right now. I may not be able to admit that to anyone else, not even Grace, but I can admit it to myself. Besides, even if I didn't win, I figure guys like Rudy will get their own in time, without me having to worry too much about it. Him losing the election would have been great, but that ain't nothing compared to what will happen to him if my dad, Tenesy, finds out that Rudy keeps my mom company at night while Dad is in prison. I'll let that ball roll on its own, though. I got other problems to worry about.

After the Clay Adams thing last fall, when I got my nose poked into his business about his missing daddy so far that I found out things I really didn't want to know, I decided I'd better keep my business to myself, unless, of course, it has to do with the law. I am still the chief of police in Deacon, Kansas, and even better than that, I've got a wife who is pure gold.

About a month ago, I passed out in the woods while I was out hunting with Daze Harper and, after a week in the hospital, found out I'm a diabetic and have a little heart problem too. I've been learning lately that I need to be more appreciative of the things I got and worry less about the other bullshit.

Grace, my wife, used to work the night shift, nursing folks in the psych ward back to some kind of normal. That's kind of how we met. She was a nurse in Tulsa when I got back from the army, my ass full of shrapnel and my head full of crap. She keeps me grounded and keeps me from doing anything stupid, and now that she's working days, she keeps me warm at night too. I pretty much have it all.

I'm cuddled up next to her, back spoon as usual, smelling her hair and listening to her snore, thinking how thankful I am that I didn't die of a heart attack in the woods, and wishing I could at least eat a cheeseburger more than once a month, when the phone rings. Being the chief does have its disadvantages. Grace doesn't move. I guess she's used to it. These days, my deputies, Jimmy, Harvey, and Angus, try to handle anything that happens at night, but sometimes, only the chief will do.

I roll over and grab the phone. It must be one of those nights. "What's up, Jimmy?" I know it's Jimmy. It's always Jimmy.

He tells me there was a big fight in the parking lot at Fat Tina's. "Rocky Martin got beat up pretty bad."

Rocky Martin is the son of the pastor of the Second Baptist Church, and he's the doorman at Tina's. "Okay, get on the horn to the sheriff. It's his jurisdiction," I say.

"The sheriff? You know he won't go out there."

"I know he won't show," I say. "I'm going to get dressed right now, but call him anyway."

I hang up and try to move slowly out of the bed, but Grace rolls over. "Something going on at Tina's?"

I grab my pants and slide in, standing at the side of the bed to zip and buckle. "Yeah, a big fight in the parking lot. It won't take long."

Tina's Gentlemen's Club sits outside the city limits and is technically in the county's jurisdiction. But the sheriff, Rudy Drown, is trying his best to close her down and pretty much ignores all the calls from there. So Tina calls me instead. She's had a little problem with drug dealers working her lot lately. She's been working to enclose the lot to better control it, and in the meantime, she relies on Angus King, who she's been friends with since college, and me. All we have to do is show up with our lights flashing, and they scatter like cockroaches. Nobody likes to go to jail. But if someone's been beat up, I'm sure the dealers are already scattered all over southeast Kansas.

As I put on my shirt and grab my service weapon, Grace rolls over in the bed. "Take your blood sugar before you go."

Damn. I hate this diabetic thing, but at least I have Grace to remind me how to stay alive. I lean over the bed and kiss her on the forehead. "Yes, ma'am. And keep the bed warm."

It's a beautiful summer night. A million stars light up the sky, and the moon is almost full. I climb in the Tahoe and head out of town, past the downtown, the city park, then the bridge that covers Beecher Creek. I look in the rearview at the large billboard, on the left side of the bridge, that says "Welcome to Deacon, First Cattle Town in Kansas" and then to the right side, at the forty-foot cross that Mrs. Beecher lights up for a few weeks every Christmas and Easter. It's dark now, but I can still see its outline.

When I was a little boy, growing up in town, I thought that cross was the greatest part of Christmas. I remember coming home from a long trip with Tenesy and Mom—don't really remember where we were—and seeing that cross lit up on the hill just as we pulled over the bridge. I knew I was home. It's been like that ever since. I don't need to see it lit, I just need to know it's still there. Deacon, Kansas. My home. The town I swore to protect and serve.

Tina's place sits almost to the state line, just past the Emerald City flea market on the corner of Dead Man's Road. That's not really the name of the road, but the locals started calling it that after Cass Adams buried her husband in her yard out there last summer. He wasn't the first to die on that same hill, of course; there was Old Man Booker that blew his house up by accident while trying to make illegal whiskey and didn't make it out in time. But after Roland, the locals thought it was spooky enough to give it a name: Dead Man's Road. It's been almost a year now. How time flies when you're finding bodies.

When I get out front of Tina's, I spot her at the back end of the gravel lot, moving sideways to squeeze in between two foreign-mades. A group of gawkers from the club has started to gather. I head that way.

There isn't much light in this part of the parking lot. Hell, there isn't much light in any of it, which I think is on purpose. Most of the guys who come out here don't want their car under a spotlight.

Tina is on the ground, facing away from me. She's wearing one of her long dresses with big purple flowers on it. Reminds me of a bedspread. Looking past her, I see Rocky in a pink T-shirt, lying on the ground, but ain't no way I can squeeze by Tina. I move around one of the cars so I can come from the other side, pushing bystanders and gawkers out of my way as I go.

"The ambulance is on its way," Tina coos at Rocky, like he's one of her kids. But I don't think he's listening. When she sees me, she says, "There was a problem out here, and I sent Rocky to check on it. When he didn't come back, I sent someone else out to find him, and this is what they found. Then I called you and an ambulance."

"Where's the ambulance?" I ask, as if she'd know.

She continues to sit with Rocky and pats his leg. "They're coming from Joplin."

I nod. Deacon has one ambulance, and if they're busy, the next closest to help is in Joplin, Missouri, thirty minutes away.

Rocky's eyes are puffy and closed, and his nose looks a lot flatter than I remember. I put my flashlight on him and swing it down his body, looking for any other damage. He tries to sit up, but I put one arm on him and tell him to lie back down. "Whoa, there, Rocky. The ambulance is coming, and I don't want you to move until they get here."

I turn toward the bouncers and point at the crowd. "Get these people out of here." I wipe the blood from my hand on my shirt. Daze Harper is standing behind Tina, trying to see over her. "Daze, go get Sammie." Sammie is the bartender and Tina's right hand at the club. Daze opens his mouth like he's going to talk back but knows better than to tell me no and turns toward the club. I pull my side radio to call Jimmy Ray.

I move a little farther back so I can talk on the radio but still keep an eye on Rocky. "I'm going to be here for a while, see if I can find out what happened. You and Harvey'll have to handle anything else that comes up."

"I just locked Randy Taylor up downstairs. Beat up his wife again," Jimmy says back. Damn, the jail's been empty for almost a month. Helluva night for the wife beater to show up.

I take a deep breath and hold down the little button again. "Tell R.T. to get comfortable."

"Anything I can help you with?" I turn around, and I'll be damned if Darnell Dix, the undersheriff, ain't standing there in his pretty county uniform.

"What are you doing here?" I might not dislike the guy, but Tina has trouble all the time, and this is the first time I can remember anyone showing up from the sheriff's office. Still, I don't have a beef with Dix. He's a young guy, pushing thirty, and I know he did his tour in the sandpit, so he has my respect for that. He's been with the sheriff's department for four years and made undersheriff just last year. His boss may be an ass and corrupt as hell, but Dix seems to stay away from the shitstorm and do his job.

"Rudy told us to keep an eye out here so he doesn't have to, so here I am, keeping an eye." He looks around and focuses on Rocky, who is now sitting up and leaned back against one of the cars. Damn, I told him to stay on his back.

I shrug. "It's your jurisdiction. I guess I can go home and crawl back in bed."

Dix cocks his head toward Rocky. "Is that Pastor Martin's kid?"

I guess that bed is going to have to wait. "Yeah. Rocky Martin. He's the doorman out here. Tina says there was some trouble in the lot, and Rocky came out to check and got clocked pretty good."

"What kind of trouble?"

I shake my head. I'm assuming it was druggies, but I ain't going to say that without someone else opening their mouth.

That doesn't take too long. "I bet I know who it was." Daze Harper is back after going for Sammie, and all he needed was an invitation to start talking. Dix pulls out a little notebook and starts writing on it.

"What's your name, sir?" he asks.

"Daisy Harper. Everyone calls me Daze, though, unless they want an ass whoopin.'"

"Did you see something, Mr. Harper?"

"No, I didn't see shit. But I got my s'picions."

Dix puts his notebook back in his pocket. "Thanks, Mr. Harper. If you remember seeing anything specific, give me a call, will ya?" He heads over closer to Rocky and Tina.

The lights from the ambulance paint the lot in red and white. I point at the ambulance then look at Daze. He crosses his arms over his chest, like he's not going to take my direction, then stomps off to guide the ambulance toward us.

"Sammie, get Tina out of the way," I say.

Tina is rubbing Rocky's leg like a puppy dog and talking to him in a calm voice. Sammie helps her get up and squeezes her out from between the cars. Damn, I don't know how she got in there in the first place.

"Who did this?" she says, shaking free of Sammie and walking toward the crowd. She's upset, and her voice is shaking, and I can tell she's mad as hell. I stand there watching the crowd, watching Tina. I've never seen Tina, not once, lose her cool, but I guess seeing someone you know beat up like that would send any woman to the edge.

"Ms. Early?" Levi Dinger catches Tina by the arm, and she spins toward him like a merry-go-round. Levi lives next door to Tina and Harlan, and he might be the only person out here big enough and strong enough to control Tina. He's also only eighteen.

"Did you see what happened, Levi?" Her whole body is shaking.

Levi lowers his head and kicks at the gravel. "No, ma'am."

He's lying.

Tina continues pushing through the crowd then turns back toward the parking lot and walks up and down, her sandals crunching on the gravel. The paramedics are all over Rocky, and I'm thinking I should have asked him who did this when I first got here.

"I hope someone saw something." I didn't realize Daze has come back to watch the paramedics and is standing close enough to hear me. I meant to say that to myself. He stands beside me and spits on the ground before saying anything.

"One of them druggies did it. Probably that little crackhead, Billy Jack. If you ask me, he should have been bagged and bricked when he was born."

Yeah, Billy Jack. His momma had a thing for those old movies. He's a cocky little ass, and everyone knows he's dealing something, but I haven't been able to catch him in the act. I haven't seen him out here before, but jerks like him have a way of hiding when they see a uniform.

"You saw him?" I'd love to catch the scrawny little ass on something like this, but everyone in town knows Daze has a history with Billy—caught him out in the woods with a gun during bow season and shot him with an arrow. Daze claimed he thought he was a deer, and Billy was too high to protest when he got to the hospital.

Daze looks at the body lying on a stretcher then back at me. "No, I ain't seen him, but he's usually out here, and he ain't nothin' but trouble." He spits on the ground again and walks toward the bar.

Jimmy Ray appears at my side, out of breath. "What can I do?" I know Jimmy likes to be in the middle of things, especially since he's getting ready to go off to more training in a few weeks. He's got a career in this, and he wants a bit of everything.

"I thought you had R.T. to take care of?" I say.

"He knows the routine. Got him in his favorite cell and thought I'd come see if you needed me." He looks around the parking lot, scanning the crowd. Jimmy's my only deputy who doesn't hang out at Tina's on his off time. He's more of a Chippendale's kind of guy. I figure he's the best deputy I've got for doing his job out here instead of trying to catch a few peeks at the girls.

"Go start talking to those gawkers. I doubt you'll get anything, but at least get all their names for Darnell Dix." I look back at the crowd, and Levi and I meet stares. "Except Levi. Tell him to be in my office tomorrow, and leave his name off the list." Jimmy heads for the crowd, and I walk toward Tina. I reach out and touch her shoulder. "Come on. I'll take you to the hospital. You need to call his family. Sammie can close the place down for the night."

"You don't have to," she says, her face a world of hurt. "I can call Harley." Tina's husband, Harlan, stays home with their two kids while Tina works at the club. I don't see the point in getting him out of bed while I'm standing right here. And besides, Tina and I have been friends since we were kids. She's one of my only friends, and I know if I needed something, she'd do whatever she could to help me.

"Come on," I say. "I think Grace sleeps better without me in the bed anyway."

Tina follows me to my truck. I open the passenger door for her, but before she gets in, she turns one more time toward the parking lot, as if she's taking it all in.

"Let's go, Tina," I say. "Darnell Dix is here, and Jimmy's asking questions. Let's go see how Rocky is."

She gets in my truck, and she's quiet as a block of cheese. She whispers something, and I can't quite hear, so I ask her what she said. She looks at me with crocodile tears running down her face. "I said, I don't think I can do this anymore."

Chapter 3
Cass

Angus's shop, Little Bit of Ink, does a lot of business. In ten years, Angus has created a name for himself as one of the best artists in the tristate area, and people come from all around just to have him stick them with inked-up needles. I sit in the front, read magazines and books, answer the phone, and sell jewelry and candles. He doesn't really need me, since most of his stuff is done by appointment, but it gets me out of the house and gives him someone to talk to.

Sonja is walking around in high heels and a pair of booty shorts, singing a song about building a snowman... in May. At night, she's a stripper at Tina's, but during the day, she apprentices with Angus, who she sees as her daddy or something. He took her in when she got beat up by some pimp up in Tulsa, and I guess he's trying to help her. That's Angus: saving the world, one Sonja at a time. She's okay in small doses, but too much and I'm sure even Angus would want to cut off his own ears. I think that's another reason he hired me: to have someone to talk to who has an IQ over 50.

The shop is slow today, which gives me some time to think. These visions I've been having bother me, and I wish they would just go away, and I hope after the baby is born, they will. But the one I had about Maryanne last night with Roland—I don't even know how to process that. I know Maryanne was in love with my husband. Hell, she had a baby with him and carried on for eighteen years until I killed him. And sure, there were times when I wished she wasn't around, but I never wished her dead. And now, she's my friend, one of the few I have, and I'd kind of like to keep it that way.

I wonder what Grams would do in this situation. I figure the best thing to do is ask her. But she doesn't know I've been seeing things, and she doesn't know I used to talk to Roland after he died, even though I'm sure she has her suspicions. I guess it's time to fess up to Grams, and I'll do that today, but first, I think I'll go check on Maryanne.

The little bell over the door rings, and a tall, skinny kid wearing a muscle tee and reeking of cheap musk walks in and heads straight to the counter. He smiles at me and looks in the jewelry cabinet without saying a word. I know I should probably ask, "Can I help you?" but this is the most fun part of my day: ignoring the customers and seeing how long it takes them to talk first. He doesn't seem to notice and points at a large gold ring in the case. "That's cool. How much?"

I'm not in the mood to play the point-and-how-much game today, unless he's flashing cash. "Is that why you're here? To buy jewelry? Because if not, just get to the point and save me having to talk any more than I have to."

His smile disappears as he looks around the shop. "I have an appointment with Sonja. Is she here?"

I look in the appointment book. *3pm. Isaac, MG Piercing*, which I know means male genitalia, what Angus prefers we not call "the family jewels." Ouch. I yell for Sonja, who yells back to give her a minute. The guy looks a little scared. "Is this your first one?" I ask.

"Uh, yeah. But I've been thinking about it for a long time. I'm doing it for my wife. Well, me, too, but mostly for her." He wipes his brow with the back of his hand and puts his face in front of the floor fan that sits next to the counter. He glances around at me and sees my belly. "You pregnant?"

Given that I'm due any day now, I'm either pregnant or swallowed a Volkswagen. What a dumb question. I rub my belly like it's painful.

"No, Sonja pierced my navel last week, and I swelled up like this. She said it's normal, but…"

"Oh, wow." He knows I'm lying and stares at me until Sonja comes to the front. When she says hello to Isaac, the smile returns.

"Four," I say to her. Sonja and I have a standing twenty-dollar bet every time she does any type of male genitalia piercing. If the customer gets excited while she's doing it, she has to wait until he is unexcited to continue. Sometimes, it takes a while for her to do something that shouldn't take thirty minutes. I think she'll have to wait four times for this guy, though now, looking at that goofy smile on his face, I wish I'd gone higher.

She giggles and flashes a mouthful of teeth at Isaac and starts talking about jewelry and penises like most people talk about what kind of pie they want from Murphy's. She's pointing at various pieces in the cabinet and throwing around terms like *Prince Albert* and *frenum*, and I know exactly what she's talking about. Part of my training was looking at pictures of different piercings and learning what they were called. Isaac has already decided, based on his extensive research on the internet and a long phone conversation with Sonja, to have a frenum, which I call Albert's Uncle Fred. The picture I saw reminded me of a little old bald man trying to lift a two-pound barbell over his head, but he just can't quite get it past his chin. Poor Uncle Fred.

He chooses an eighteen-karat gold barbell, and Sonja winks at me. Usually they choose steel or titanium, which gets them out of here for around a hundred bucks, but this kid is going to spend four times that for Uncle Fred. I guess I should be nicer.

"Okay, well, let's go and get started," she says. "I'll have to figure out what size you need, and we'll go from there."

"Size? It's not a one-size-fits-all?" the kid asks.

Sonja is walking and talking. Isaac blindly follows.

"We need to take into consideration swelling, erection room, and whether you are circumcised…"

I shake my head. So much for his internet research.

He stops and turns back toward me. "Swelling?"

I rub my belly and wiggle my eyebrows.

Sonja puts a hand on his arm. "It'll be fine. I'll explain everything in detail before I do anything. And you can always change your mind."

"No. Let's do this. It'll be... fun," Isaac says.

I'm not so sure that's the right word for it. I perch myself on the stool in front of the counter and grab a magazine while Sonja and Isaac take up camp in one of the three partitioned areas in the shop.

The little bell rings again, and I look up to see Angus. He's wearing his cop uniform, which makes me laugh. Sonja is dressed like Daisy Duke, Angus is a cop, and I look like a Sumo wrestler. It's like never-ending Halloween in here. "I thought you were out saving the world," I say. I know Angus likes to check on Sonja and me when we're alone, but really, he doesn't have to. We haven't killed anyone yet.

"I've got an appointment I set up several weeks ago. I don't want to disappoint my customers," he says. "And besides, I need a break."

I get off my stool slowly and damn near fall over as Peanut moves in the opposite direction that I do. Angus reaches out and catches me from falling into the glass display case. "You look like you could use one too. After Sonja and I are done, we'll close up for the day. I need to go check on Tina." He looks at his watch and sighs.

Damn. That vision I had. "Is she okay?"

He cocks his head slightly as he answers. "She's fine. You seem so concerned."

I shrug. "I'm just asking."

"There was some trouble last night at the club, and she's pretty upset about it. One of the bouncers got beat up, and—"

I wave him off. The guy in the wood chipper. Another vision confirmed.

Angus is usually as cheery as a Christmas elf, but his smile is missing, and he has one of those big lines running down between his eyes. I doubt that the added police work he's doing for Benny is stressing him out, and I can't think of much that he does that would cause him strife. But he is dating Maryanne, and I know that has to be challenging at times.

When they first met, Maryanne didn't exactly like him. I think his size turned her off—she had always been used to men taller than her, not a foot shorter. But once she got to know him, she realized she had been gauging men by the wrong ruler her entire life. Angus treats her with respect, makes her laugh, and to hear her tell it, makes mad, passionate love to her without asking for anything but the same in return. I think it's the first time in her life that she's been faithful for more than a weekend.

"What's wrong?" I ask him. Since I met Angus, he's been a good person for me to talk to about things I don't normally like to put out there. I figure the least I can do is act interested if he has something he needs to talk about too.

"Maryanne seems very anxious about telling Shaylene she's moving in with me, and I think I know why," he says.

"Because she's a drama queen? You already knew that when you asked her to move in, so this shouldn't be too much of a surprise."

He shakes his head and has a real serious look on his face, so I figure I should just listen and try not to say much.

"She's worried about the time commitments to school, work, and... well, us. But I told her that 'us' is just fine, and I'm not going to get upset because she's doing something for herself. It's a time commitment, I know, but I'm happy with the leftovers. I thought when I told her that if she doesn't want to work once she moves in with me, that's fine by me, everything would be fine, but it's not."

Angus has a lot of money—not that many people know that, but I do. I got nosy one night when there was nobody in the shop and found some statements from an investment company. He's rolling in it. Since he bought the land on Booker Hill from me, he started construction on a house, a big house, and it won't even dent his investment accounts. Feeding Maryanne while she goes to school won't hurt it either.

"What does this have to do with telling Shaylene?" He was losing me. With most people, I'd just walk away, but Angus is one of my few friends, and I know I'm supposed to listen.

"I think moving in with me, and me taking care of her, is a lot like being married, but without it being official. And maybe she doesn't want to tell Shaylene unless it is, you know, official."

I shake my head. Oh no, I think I know where this is going. "You didn't ask her to marry you, did you?"

"Not yet." He pulls a small box out of his pocket and shows me a diamond bigger than Kansas. "Look, I know it's only been five months, but we aren't in our twenties. We don't have to spend months playing hard to get to save anyone's reputation. We enjoy being together, and five months is a pretty good run for both of us. And I know what I want."

"Maybe it isn't marriage that's bothering her but the idea of moving out to the Hill that has spooked her." When I was married to Roland and living in a shack on the Hill, Maryanne was having an affair with my husband, and I'm sure if Roland had volunteered to build her a big house out there, she'd have been happy to move. But since I killed him and buried him there, she may not like the idea as much.

Angus smiles. "She says the place may be cursed. I told her it isn't. It's a beautiful piece of land where something bad happened to have occurred. Well, bad, depending on your perspective. I told her I had it blessed and all the demons have been removed."

I know that isn't true. I've been slowly cleaning out the barn on the Hill since the weather has gotten warmer, and I know better. The two men who died on that hill, Roland and Old Man Booker, are still around.

I point at the ring he still holds in his hand. "So when do you plan to do that?"

"Shaylene gets here tomorrow. So, I think while she's here, maybe this weekend." He smiles, but I can tell it's forced. He's scared, and I don't blame him.

Although Maryanne and I have had some pretty serious differences over the years, I still call her my friend. But Maryanne is like a lot of women—they say they want a good man, and yet they go after the bad ones. When a good one comes along, they hesitate, or screw around and lose him all together. After living with Roland for twenty years, I knew Clay was a good one and jumped right on that. Maryanne waited on Roland for those same twenty years, and now he's dead, and she's got a live one, right here, offering her everything she ever wanted. If I didn't know she was getting ready to die, I'd say she'd probably find a way to fuck up her relationship with Angus. But all I can do is shake my head.

I don't know what else to say to Angus. I certainly don't want to tell him about my visions. Thankfully, the little bell over the door clangs and saves me from having to say anything. Nick Dixon, my sister's ex, walks in and sees me behind the counter and lets out a loud groan. I hiss at him.

"Oh, I see you two know each other!" Angus's wide smile is back; he has shifted into Angus King, Tattoo Artist mode.

"Yeah, he was married to my sister a long time ago." I was a teenager then, and although I've never liked many people, I especially didn't like Nick. He was rude to my Grams and treated Lola like baggage. I cut the crotch out of his favorite jeans and put petroleum jelly on the door handles of his car about once a week. One night, he passed out at Grams's place, and I wrote *ASS* in big letters with black Sharpie on his forehead and on both cheeks. It took a week for him to scrub it all off.

"We weren't married, we just played house," Nick corrects me. I shrug. Lola had a long string of losers in her early years—some she married, some she didn't. I get them all confused.

"Well," Angus says, "let's get started. This one is going to take a while." Nick follows Angus to his cubicle, which he keeps cleaner than a surgical room. I can hear them talking about the tattoo Nick is getting, some kind of gun on his bicep, and he wants to make sure it's healed by Friday, when he goes off to some shooting competition. Figures.

I walk to the back, time for my third pee of the hour, and stick my tongue out at Nick as I do. The bathroom door is unlocked, so I walk in, and there stands Isaac, trying to get his "swelling" to go down so Sonja can start on his frenum. "Oh, come on!" I say. Not what I wanted to see today. I walk to the front, telling Angus I'm leaving, and grab my keys off the counter.

Angus has an engagement ring, and I see a random penis. This day can't get any weirder.

I JUMP OUT OF THE TRUCK at Maryanne's house, run in without knocking, open the bathroom door, and there stands her friend and the school principal, Bobby Leo, pissing a stream. "Doesn't anybody lock the bathroom door in this town?" I scream as I limp toward Maryanne's second bathroom, off her bedroom. I finally make it to the toilet with only a little dribble. That's the second penis I've seen in the past fifteen minutes, and I sure as hell didn't care to see even one today.

When I come out, Bobby and Maryanne are sitting at the kitchen table. His face is white as his skinny little ass was. Maryanne is laughing. I don't think it's funny.

"I am so sorry," he says without looking at me.

"Well, you damn sure should be. Who doesn't lock the bathroom door?" I start digging in Maryanne's refrigerator and see a jar of sweet pickles. I grab it and sit down at the table. "Do you have any peanut butter?"

Bobby is the principal at Central Elementary School, where Maryanne works as a teacher. Since Shaylene went off to college, and with Roland off to God's Acre, Maryanne doesn't have many people to talk to. I try, but I'm not always around much. And of course, there's Angus, but sometimes you need someone to talk to that you aren't sleeping with. She and Bobby seem to be becoming good friends. He reminds me of that guy who used to talk about his neighborhood to kids and wore those sweaters. I can picture Bobby talking like that with the kids at the school. Mr. Leo's Neighborhood.

"I should go," he says. He still hasn't looked at me, and that's fine. I've seen enough of him for a lifetime. He grabs his lunch box off the table, an old tin one with a picture of Captain America on it.

"Captain America? I figure you for more of a Wonder Woman type," I say.

"Wonder Woman?" he says. "No, she's a DC character. Marvel characters are the best. In fact—"

"I was just kidding, Bobby." Jeez, it might not have been a good penis joke, but it was the best I got.

Maryanne gives me a look and walks him to the door. He's still apologizing for what he's calling "the mishap," and I shake my head. No wonder the guy still lives with his mother.

When she comes back, I have to ask. "You aren't sleeping with him, are you?"

"No, I am not, as if it were any of your business." She still has on her clothes from school, a pair of navy pants and a white shirt with a matching navy sweater. Her hair is tied up in a neat little bun, and her makeup is light and perfect. "You know my heart belongs to Gus."

It wasn't exactly her heart I was referring to.

She grabs a jar of peanut butter from the cupboard and a spoon from the drawer and hands them to me as she sits down. "How are you feeling?"

"Aside from having to pee every five minutes, pretty good." I dip the spoon in the peanut butter and smear it on a sweet pickle. Maryanne curls her nose up at me but doesn't say anything about it. I point my pickle toward the door. "You sure you aren't getting a little friendly with the comic book boy?"

She brushes a piece of imaginary lint from her sweater. "Not even if he were the Incredible Hulk."

"Incredible Hulk? If that thing is green, I wouldn't go near it. And it's not, by the way—green or incredible." We both start laughing the way women do when they're talking about men and their penises. It's good to laugh.

"Did he steal that lunch box from one of the kids?" A grown man with a cartoon lunch box. I wonder what Clay would say if I bought him one for work.

She waves a hand toward the door. "He's got several. Collects all things superhero. He dressed like Thor for Halloween last year, and let's just say his hammer wasn't quite big enough to pull it off."

Maryanne is my best friend. Sure, she was sleeping with my husband and had his kid, but still, she's the best friend I have. Since she's been seeing Angus, she seems pretty happy, but when I look at her now, I notice she's shaking a little and looks out the window a lot. "Are you feeling okay?"

She gives me the same cocked-head look that Angus did. "I'm fine. Why?"

Because I think you're going to die in the next few days, and I'm hoping it's not going to be today. No. I can't say that. I shake my head. *Forget about it, Cass, until you talk to Grams.*

"Angus told me you're freaked out about telling Shaylene you're moving in with him, which is stupid," I say. Nothing like getting right to the point. "She likes Angus, and he's all you've been talking about for months, and I know he's in love with you, so what's the problem?"

She rubs the back of her neck. "Telling Shaylene makes it... real."

"So it isn't telling Shaylene, it's the moving-in-with-him part," I say. "Now that you already told him you would, you're thinking maybe that's not such a good idea. Figures."

"It's a big step, Cass." Maryanne puts her hands on top of mine, which pisses me off because I want a bite of pickle. "I mean, I want a relationship, and I do love Angus, but I'm not sure if I want to make it so permanent. Moving in is... exclusive." Maryanne is like a lot of women—they think they want a fairy tale, then when someone comes along and is ready to give them the world, they aren't quite sure if it's the world they want. Or maybe they just enjoy the idea of the foreplay, the romancing part, but when it's time to actually settle down and be happy, they discover that's not what they really want either. She lets go of my hand, and I stick the pickle in my mouth. Sweet, sour, and peanut butter.

"You're already exclusive." Before seeing Angus, Maryanne was looser than an old bolt. She went out every weekend and found a different man. But that woman is gone, or at least I thought she was. She's looking out the window still and not saying a word. *Damn.*

I point my pickle at her. "Please tell me you haven't been screwing around on Angus." I never cared much that Maryanne went out for her weekend Romeos. She was single, so what difference did it make if she wanted to have fun? But once you're with someone steady, cheating is one of the worst things you can do to them. It hurts. I know that from experience. And I hate to even think about her hurting Angus.

"I..." She shakes her head and takes a deep breath.

Damn. "Really, Maryanne? You're cheating on him?"

"No! I mean, just once. A month ago, when he went to Boston to see his parents. I was lonely, and—"

"He asked you to go with him, and you told him you couldn't. Lonely, my ass." I want to stuff my pickle down her throat until she chokes. Maybe the reason I had that vision is because I'm actually the one who kills her. "It wasn't with Comic Boy, was it?"

"Bobby? No, I told you, he's only a friend. It doesn't matter who it was with, and it was one time, and I do love Angus, but I wanted to make sure, I guess, and it wasn't even any fun, but I did it. And Angus is so good to me, and I wish it hadn't have happened. I don't want him to know." She covers her face with her hands, but I don't feel a bit sorry for her.

I think about the big-ass ring Angus is carrying around in his pocket, and I want to strangle Maryanne about now. "Well, he's ready to go the distance for you, so I think you need to tell him the truth so he can change his mind if he wants to." It comes out all garbled as I stuff the rest of the pickle in my mouth.

"That's the problem. I don't want him to change his mind. I do love him, and I want to move in with him. I made a big mistake, though, and I don't think I can tell him."

I screw the lid on the peanut butter and put it in the refrigerator. I've got to get to Grams, and I've heard more than I wanted to, anyway. "Well, I'm not going to tell him. But if you lie to him, there's always a chance he's going to find out. Then what?"

She sits up tall and lifts her chin. "He won't find out. You won't say anything, and the only other way he could find out is if I tell him. I've kept secrets before, I can do it again."

I shake my head as I walk toward the door. She kept the secret about Shaylene being Roland's kid for eighteen years, so I know she can keep her mouth shut. But like with Shaylene, all secrets eventually come to light, even if some take a while.

GRAMS'S HOUSE IS JUST a short drive from Maryanne's. I park my truck behind her titty-pink Cadillac. When my feet land on her front porch, I stop for a minute to take a breath and feel a sense of relief wash over me. This is the house I grew up in, with Lola, Grams, and Grandpa Jack. A lot of bad things happened here, like when my mother hung herself when I was five, but a lot of good things did too, and no matter where I go, this will always be home.

Something sweet and cinnamon-y wafts from the kitchen as I walk in, and I know Grams has been baking. My mouth waters as I think about stuffing myself with a huge homemade cinnamon roll. I go straight to the kitchen—no Grams, but a large baking dish of bread pudding sits on her cooling pad. Even better.

"Grams!" I call out as I grab a bowl and a serving spoon and help myself to the bread pudding.

"I'll be right there," she says from the bathroom. "Grab some bread pudding. It's fresh out of the oven."

I'm a step ahead of you, Grams.

On the small kitchen table, three different decks of tarot cards are lined up neatly in a row, and I sit on the opposite side so I don't disturb them. Grams must have something heavy on her mind to be consulting three separate decks. The covers of the three decks—one dark brown with a yellow sun in the middle, another gold with nothing but a simple green border, and the third, one I've known since childhood, blue, white, and black in a plaid pattern—all mean something different to Grams. But I know the real stuff, the pictures that tell Grams's stories, are on the other side.

Grams has always been able to see things, and sometimes she's right, and sometimes she's not. She told my sister, Lola, in high school that she'd one day have a lot of money, and three husbands later, she finally married a rich one. She was right that time. She also told me, and everyone else in town, that I didn't kill my husband, Roland. She was dead wrong that time. I stuff a large forkful of bread pudding in my mouth and focus on the plaid tarot card deck. I think Clay has a shirt just like that one.

"How's the pudding?" Grams smiles as she sets a white candle on the table in front of the three decks. A cleansing candle. I remember that too.

"Reery goo," I say with my mouth full. I point my fork at the decks of cards and raise an eyebrow at her.

She waves a hand dismissively in the air. "Oh, you know me. Just playing with my cards." She doesn't look me in the eye when she says that, and I notice that big crevice in the middle of her forehead, what she calls her "thinking line," is deeper than a country well. She puts the cards back in their little packs, careful not to disturb their placement, and drops them into the pocket of her apron.

I put my fork down, suddenly not feeling too much like stuffing my face with bread pudding, and reach across the table and put my hand on top of hers. She's shaking.

"Grams, you got me real worried now. What the hell did you see in those cards?"

She finally looks at me, and I swear I can see straight to her insides, and I know she's hurting. I want to tell her everything is going to be okay, but I think I know what she's upset about, and it's not going to be okay. It sucks. I take a deep breath and let it out slowly, then I squeeze her hand just a little. "I know. Is there anything we can do to stop it?"

She tilts her head and gives me a little smile, a knowing smile. "You've seen things," she says. She doesn't ask it, she says it like she knows it to be true. I nod. My big secret, and Grams knew all along. Figures.

"Since I've been pregnant. Just a few things, but they've all come true. And this thing with Maryanne..." This thing. We both know what that means, but I can't seem to say it out loud.

She looks at me for a second without saying anything. Then a tear trails down her face and hangs on her chin before dropping to her housecoat. "Maryanne." She's nodding and shaking her head at the same time, if that can even be done. "It's Maryanne. I couldn't tell who, just that someone close is..."

She's smiling and frowning and crying, and I realize that she thought it might be me. Or Lola. We're her girls, all she has in this world, and she's relieved it's not us—happy, even—but it's Maryanne. I get up and go around the table and wrap her in a big hug. It's been a while since I really hugged Grams, and she feels so soft and warm I don't want to let her go. "What do we do, Grams?"

"Nothing," she says.

I love my Grams, and I respect her, but I'm not so sure I like her plan. I pull a chair next to her and sit down, wanting to talk but not wanting to distance myself from her. "Nothing? That isn't going to save her." *And I don't want her dead.*

"It just doesn't work that way," she says. "We don't get to decide what happens, we just see it sometimes."

I can't accept that. "No. It isn't a science, and you've been wrong before." I said that without thinking. I never told Grams the truth about Roland's death; I just never had the heart to. She was convinced, and told everyone in town, that I didn't kill him. But I did. And I don't really want to tell her now.

"When have I been wrong?" she says.

I hate to lie, and with most people, I tell them exactly what I think, regardless of whether they like it or not. But I just can't tell Grams. I just can't. "I mean, surely you've been wrong before?"

She lets out a sigh and gives me one of her fake smiles. "You're right. Maybe I'm wrong this time."

But I know she doesn't believe that. And neither do I.

Chapter 4
Benny

I sit down and prop my feet up on my worn walnut desk. I'm looking forward to a nice quiet day of paperwork at the station. I take a sip from my coffee, black and steaming, and let out a long sigh. After last night, I'm not in the mood for any more excitement.

I stayed with Tina at the hospital until Darnell Dix showed up. Rocky was in surgery, broken jaw and nose, and he couldn't talk, so Dix left his card and said he'd be back in the morning. At least it wasn't that arrogant son of a bitch Rudy Drown. He doesn't give a shit. Never has. What an asshole.

I know it's none of my business. That club is outside of my jurisdiction. But it's a little more personal than that. I'm not saying we have Sunday dinner or go play bingo once a week, but Tina and I are friends. We both have spouses that we spend most of our time with, but sometimes, it's good to have someone other than Grace to just shoot the shit with. We respect each other, and I don't think in our professions, either one of us sees much of that. Tina and Harlan are good people, regardless of the type of business they're in. One thing I've learned in this world is that if you're good at something, you can make money at it. Just happens Tina is good at running a strip joint. So be it.

"I'm going out to get R.T. a piece of pie at Murphy's. You want anything?" Jimmy Ray sticks his head in. He's been working for me for the past two years. He's a good kid, never complains and works hard. I think he was hoping that I'd make sheriff so he could move up, but he doesn't seem to be too upset that I didn't win. He's graduating from the community college next week with a two-year degree in criminal justice, and I'm sending him off to the Kansas Law Enforcement Training Center over in Hutchinson for more training the week after that. He's one of those kids who's going to find a way to move up, and damn if he might take my job from me one day.

"Since when do we take prisoners a piece of pie?" I ask. Jimmy's problem is he cares too much. I know that doesn't sound like much of a problem, but sometimes you gotta be a hard-ass. I'm not sure Jimmy has that in him. "What else we got going on?"

"Mrs. Meadows lost one of her dogs again. This time it's Schmegel, and she says that if Schmegel stays out too long, his allergies will start acting up and he'll sneeze for a week. So it's pretty serious." I shake my head. I've chased enough of Mrs. Meadows's Chihuahuas to not find it funny anymore. But it's still fun to mess with Jimmy. "So why are you going for pie when Schmegel's respiratory health is in danger?"

"Well, I..."

The sound of yelling in the hallway makes me lose my balance, and I spill hot coffee all over my pant leg. *Shit*. My chair hits the floor with a loud thud, and I get up fast to see what the hell is going on. As I walk to the doorway, I see Harvey Cox coming down the hall with Billy Jack in handcuffs.

"He ran a red light, and I pulled him over. Funny thing, when I ran his license, sheriff has a warrant out on him for hot checks." Harvey is smiling and has his chest puffed out like a prized rooster at the county fair.

Billy looks at me and says, "This is racial profiling. I want my lawyer." He gives me a shit-eating grin.

Billy was raised right here in Deacon, and as far as I know, he ain't never been farther than the white side of Kansas City. But for some reason, a few years ago, he decided he was the next Eminem or some shit and walks around with his pants hanging off his ass and making little hand signs that don't mean a damn thing.

"Take him downstairs, Harvey. I'll call the sheriff."

Harvey grabs him kinda rough, which I kinda like, and turns him around, pushing him toward the stairwell that leads to the basement. "Hey," Billy says, "you can't keep me in your dungeon."

"We're not keeping you, just holding you until the sheriff gets here. He can do whatever the hell he wants with you."

Jimmy Ray is still standing in the hall. "Go find Schmegel," I say. "R.T. can have pie when he and his wife stop fighting."

Billy's still yelling as Harvey opens the door to the jail. "Always want to hold a brotha down. I got rights, you know!"

I head back toward the office. "Yeah, you got rights, Billy. But here's a news flash. You ain't black." As I walk by my desk, the phone begins to ring. I grab the receiver and put it to my ear. "Cloud here."

"Please hold for the sheriff," the sweet voice on the other end of the line says.

"Please hold for the sheriff," I say in my best girlie voice. He's the sheriff of Cherokee County, Kansas, not the governor.

"Sheriff Drown," he says after making me wait a full minute.

"I know who it is. You called me, Rudy. What do you want?" I've known Rudy Drown since I was a kid. He used to run around with Tenesy and my mom and Freddy Adams, Roland and Clay's dad. Freddy ran off when we were all little, but Rudy was always around. He was a dick. Hasn't really changed much.

"Hey there, Benny. Just thought I'd touch base with you about last night. You get any info from any of those witnesses I need to know about?" Rudy's also keeping my mom warm at night while my dad is in prison. That pisses me off more than anything, but it's hard not to laugh about it right now. Tenesy gets out next month, and the storm that's going to rain on Rudy when he figures it all out will make Dorothy's trip to Oz seem like a flight to Paris in a first-class cabin.

"Dix was at the hospital, so why don't you ask him? I got Billy Jack in holding, though, waiting for you to come and get his sorry ass."

"Billy Jack? That little wannabe homeboy? What do I want with him?"

"Your office has a warrant out for hot checks. My guys picked him up."

"Huh," he says.

Huh. That's it?

"I'll send someone over to get him. Say, we got another little problem going on. Might could use your help with."

Drown's idea of "might could use your help with" usually means he wants me to take care of something that he feels is beneath him. I don't say anything, just wait for him to continue.

"Got some church ladies out at that strip joint carrying signs around. Quite a little crowd gathering right out there on the highway. Think you could go out there and take a look-see?"

"I got my own stuff going on right now, Rudy. Why would I want to go out there?"

"Well, the women came from the Second Baptist Church of Deacon. I figure your town, your ladies."

Shit. I know who most of those ladies are, and I got a feeling I know who is ramrodding that whole operation. "Okay, I'll swing out there and see what's going on. Don't forget to send someone after this little ass. I don't want him stinkin' up my building any more than he already has."

"Will do. And Benny? You might want to make sure you look pretty going out there. I hear the news folk are on their way. You might get yourself on TV."

I look down at my uniform, where a dark-brown stain from my coffee has already dried on the light blue. Shit.

Chapter 5
Tina

Sammie sets a cup of coffee on the patio table and sits down next to me. We don't say anything for a few minutes, we just sit and look off the deck of my house and watch the Spring River flow by like it has for hundreds of years. I raise the cup and blow on the coffee and, closing my eyes, take a drink. I feel a familiar brush against my leg and look down. It's Calico, but I don't have the energy to reach down and pet her.

"What did the hospital say?" The incident with Rocky last night was not the first incident we've had in the parking lot in the past few months, but it certainly was one of the worst.

"He'll be fine." Broken nose, two black eyes, and a dozen stitches on his forehead. I sure hope he doesn't quit. I probably should be more concerned about if he'll sue. I let out a long sigh and take another sip of my coffee.

Since I opened the club fifteen years ago, I haven't had much trouble at all until recently. I had a good business plan going in and decided the only way to make it successful was to keep it clean. Of course, it is a gentlemen's club, so the rules had to be clearly defined. The laws on a club like Fat Tina's are very cut and dry: As long as the bar is open, topless is as far as the girls can go. They can do lap dances, but only with their clothes on, even though "clothes" can consist of G-strings and bras. And absolutely no paid-for sex. That would be prostitution, and I am definitely not a madam. What the girls do after hours is their own business, but they know better than to do it on my property. Sure, I pass out condoms, but that's just marketing. The bank passes out ink pens, but they don't expect you to make a grocery list while sitting in their lobby.

I had to do a lot of research to figure out how to work the laws to my advantage and still provide the girls an opportunity to get enough tips to make it worth their while. I make a lot of money from the bar and the cover charge, but at one o'clock in the morning, we close the bar to anything but soft drinks, and those last few hours are when the girls make their big tips. Between one and three, I count my money in the back while the girls clean those pockets out up front. It's been quite lucrative for all of us.

But with any lucrative business endeavor, you're going to have the small entrepreneurs who try to ride on your coattails. Bill Gates has a million basement bandits trying to capitalize on his work, and I have drug dealers in my parking lot.

"We've got to find a way to get that lot under control," I say. Or close it down. I don't want to say this to anyone, but I've been at it fifteen years, and lately I've been thinking that maybe it's time to do something different. Something that doesn't involve drug dealers, bouncers getting beat up, and half-naked women. The boys are getting older, old enough to know what their mother does for a living, and I'm not sure if a strip club, even one that makes a lot of money, is setting a good example for them.

When Roland Adams was my head bouncer, he had it under control. I never asked what exactly he did; I guess now I should have. But I really wanted to make sure I was clean, and I figured if I didn't know, I would be protected if anything major ever went down. In hindsight, that wasn't the best policy. Sure, I knew there were still a few drug deals going on in the lot, but it was all very civil, for lack of a better word, and kept very low-key.

Now, Roland has been dead a year, and everything has changed. It's as if without Roland out there making sure everything was done under the table, the dealers have decided it's easier to be open, even aggressive, about marketing their products. And whereas a year ago we had maybe three or four regulars in the lot, now there are guys coming from all over to sell to my customers; and drug dealing is not a business that takes kindly to new competition.

I blink several times and try to focus on Tabby, sitting on the railing of the porch, licking her paw and rubbing her ear with it. I sit my coffee cup down a little too hard, causing coffee to spill over the top and on the tile of the table.

Sammie wipes the table with her napkin. "Why don't you stay home with Harlan and the boys tonight? I can handle the club." Sammie is my right hand. Sure, Harley helps me out, and I've got a few good employees that I can count on, but Sammie is different.

Shortly after Angus moved to town, Harley, Angus, and me started working on the fishing shack that we lived in. We figured we could make it a nice little cottage-style home with our own labor and a small investment then build the big house once we paid off the mortgage for the club. The three of us lived there, Harlan worked during the day, and Angus and I worked at the club and worked on the house in our spare time.

One night, Angus brought Sammie home. At first, Harley and I didn't know what to think, but neither of us have ever been the type to judge. As we got to know her, the fact that she dressed and acted like a man wasn't even a point of question. That's just Sammie. And she was a working machine. She could out-hammer Harley and hauled lumber like a horse. While Harley and I worked our jobs, Angus and Sammie finished the house and turned it into a cozy little two-bedroom log cabin.

Angus and Sammie never had a relationship. She worked at a bar he likes to frequent in Tulsa, and they grew to be friends. When he realized she had a lot of potential and wasn't going anywhere, he want-ed to help. That's Angus. And I trust his judgment, so after the shack was finished, I offered her a job. She tends bar and doesn't cheat me. She doesn't flirt with the customers or the girls, and her stuttering keeps her from saying too much. She's always got her eyes open, and if some-thing's going on, I can count on Sammie to let me know. She's worked for me for ten years now, and I pay her well. Angus invests her mon-ey like he does for all of us, and considering what my savings looks like now, I can assume that Sammie is doing just fine. But she sticks around. Kind of like family.

"Thanks, Sammie." Blacky jumps in my lap and gives me a long me-ow. I rub him absently, and he jumps back down.

"And Gus will be there too. He's called some of his friends from Tulsa to help keep the lot under control tonight. It'll be fine."

I try not to smile as I picture a foot patrol of small wrestlers in my parking lot, running between cars and cracking dealers at the knees.

"I appreciate it. But you know, I think I need to make sure I'm there tonight. Just to let everyone know I'm not afraid." Even if I am having second thoughts about my choice of business, I still have to make sure the club is up and running tonight. As they say, the show must go on.

Angus has been my best friend since college. When we graduated, we had hopes of going to New York together with our MBAs and get-ting a job on Wall Street. I couldn't do it. I've always been a small-town girl, and the thought of being in a city of that size made my blood pres-sure rise. And truth be told, at that time, I didn't have the confidence in myself that I needed to make it work.

Angus, however, had to take a chance. He was a natural, a master with the markets, and I used to tease him and say he was like a little black Will Rogers—never met a man he didn't like. He had a job in a securities firm in the Twin Towers and wore his three-piece suits every day. That, of course, was before the towers fell. Afterward, he showed up in Deacon for the opening of my club and never left. I tried to give him a job, but he wouldn't take it. He drove to Tulsa every day to work with a guy who's one of the top tattoo artists in the country. After five years, Angus opened his own shop in Deacon and has been inking the locals ever since. He doesn't make a lot of money, but what he does make, he knows how to turn it into more. And he's happy. That's really all that matters.

"Well, we're all here for you. You know that," Sammie says.

Velvet gives me one of her piercing high meows, as if agreeing. I open my mouth to thank them both when Angus walks in, flashing that smile that could melt a glacier. He kisses Sammie and me both on the cheek and rubs Candy as she jumps up for her daily acknowledgment. He looks up at me with big brown eyes. "Any change, Sis?"

I shake my head. Angus has a nickname for everyone; mine is Sis. Since neither of us have siblings, it's appropriate. I can't think of anyone I'd rather have for a brother. "Sammie tells me your friends are going to help out at the club for a bit. I appreciate that."

"No problem," he says. "Sebastian sounded pretty excited about it." Then he snaps his fingers. "Say, I wonder if Harlan would mind if we used a few of those cameras he has? If we can catch someone in the act of something, maybe a photographic record would be good for the police?"

Harley has cameras of every shape and size. When he was a boy, he swears he saw an alien spacecraft land out in a field behind his mother's house on Grand Lake, and no one believed him. He's been tracking UFOs ever since and says the next time, he'll get a video. I guess we all have our odd little hobbies, and that's the one he shares with our boys, Eb and Augie. His other hobby, which involves a collection of porn that would make Larry Flynt blush, is his alone. He has a private viewing room that's locked up tighter than Fort Knox.

"I'm sure he wouldn't mind, Angus. But I'm not quite sure the sheriff cares much about what happened last night. If it were Benny, it would be a different story. But it's Rudy Drown."

"Well, whatever I can do. Just say the word, Sis." He sits down at the table on the other side of Sammie. She gets up and goes to the kitchen to get him some coffee. Tabby jumps on his lap, and he pets her in long, gentle strokes.

"Shouldn't you be at the shop?" I appreciate that Angus is here to check on me, but I know he has his own responsibilities. First is his tattoo shop, but he also has his uniform on, so he's probably supposed to be working for Benny right now.

"Sonja and I are done for the day, and I sent Cass home early. And I needed a cup of your coffee," he says.

Cass Adams. Other than at Roland's funeral, I've only seen Cass a handful of times. Years ago, when I first got back from college, we worked together at the truck stop. I kind of think she liked me, in her way, which was that she didn't dislike me. Of course, she verbally abused me just like she did everyone else, but I didn't let it get to me, and she didn't seem to find her actions inappropriate at all. I guess we all know for sure now that she really does have some mental problems. Back then, we just assumed it.

It's hard for me to imagine that Angus and she have become friends. I know when they first met, the fact that he was a dwarf was quite a novelty for her. He says he appreciated her openness and was glad she asked questions, even if they were blunt. She works in his tattoo shop a few mornings a week, a way to get him a little help and her to get out of the house, at least until her baby is born. I guess it's good for both of them.

Angus is what I call a collector of people. Everyone likes him, but he's drawn to those that others tend to dismiss. Maybe I was his first, then Sammie, then Sonja, and now Cass Adams. He tries to find the good in everyone and helps anyone he can. It's a quality that many claim to have but few actually possess.

But he isn't perfect; no man is. Angus is good and just and caring because he carries his own scars. Being born a dwarf, he's had his share of feeling like the outcast. He told me once, in college, that he likes to make others feel welcome, because he hasn't always felt that way himself. He hides his insecurities well, but I know they are there.

"Is she doing okay?" Even though I haven't seen her, I live in a small town, and news of anything travels pretty fast. If it's something really interesting, it's like lightning. Last November, Cass Adams, the woman who buried her husband in their yard and was accused of killing him and now lives with his brother, found out she was pregnant. Then she did exactly what someone would expect of her; she got a dog.

"Doing well. Ornery as ever and cute as a bug with her belly all swelled out, but she's healthy and due any day. I'll tell her you asked." I'm sure Cass wouldn't care that I asked about her. But I am concerned—not that her having a child is any of my business, but she's my age, in her late thirties, and I know that many times, complications happen. I'd hate to see that happen to her and Clay.

Angus quits stroking Tabby and takes a sip of his coffee. He looks off absently toward the river, and I know something else is on his mind. I give him a full minute to start talking, but he's a man, and sometimes, they need a little prompting. "I know that look of worry on your face isn't about the club."

He nods, reaches into his pocket, and pulls out a little ring box and lays it on the table. "I'm having second thoughts."

Last week, Angus told me he intended to ask Maryanne Spencer to marry him. My first reaction was to tell him to run back to New York. But I know he really loves her, and who am I to say that she hasn't changed her ways since they've been dating? I don't really care that they have only known each other a short time. My concern is her history. I don't want to see Angus hurt. But he's a grown man, and a smart one, and if this is what he really wants, then I told him he should go for it. Life is too short to *want*.

"What happened?"

He lets out a deep breath. "Nothing, really. Maybe I'm just afraid she'll say no."

"She's already moving in with you, so..."

"I know. It's just... Damn, I hate to even say this out loud, but what if I'm not enough for her? I know what she used to be like, and I swear, if she cheats on me, I'll lose my mind."

I wish I had some good advice for him, but I don't. I hate to say nothing, and I start to open my mouth with some cliché about taking a chance when I'm saved by Harley. He puts his arms around me from behind. I didn't even hear him walk out on the porch. "Sammie told me that she and Angus are trying to give you the night off. Take it. After we put the boys to bed, we'll go down to the dock and watch the river flow like we used to."

It's not enough to say I love my husband. When the club started requiring more of my time, he dropped his work to part-time and chose to stay home with the boys. I'm here with them until around eight each evening, but it never seems to be enough. Maybe I do just need a break.

"What if it rains?" When Harley and I first started living at the fishing shack, we used to go to the dock and make love in the rain. The river rushing beside and under us, the storm raging above us—it was the most amazing sex I've ever had.

He kisses my neck. "All the better."

The phone rings in the house, and Sammie answers it. My coffee is a little warm now, and I drink it and look at the river. I can take a night off. Why not? I have to remember, I own the club, it doesn't own me. I turn my head to Harley just as Sammie walks back on the porch. She doesn't sit down. "That was Benny on the phone. Looks like we got some trouble at the club."

"Trouble? It's only four o'clock." The club doesn't open until eight, and unless the place is on fire, I can't imagine what kind of trouble we could have.

"Picketers. A whole bunch of women from one of the churches in town. Daze Harper's wife is leading the pack."

Calico is rubbing on my leg again, and this time, I pick her up and put her in my lap. I rub her soft fur and listen for her low purr. I know some people may think I have too many cats, but how many is really too many? I keep them around for times like this. When I've got too much going on, I can lose myself in their I-don't-care attitude, and it gives me time to think.

I've got an employee in the hospital who's been beaten up by drug dealers. A religious group picketing my club. A dwarf army on its way from Tulsa to guard my lot. And a family that needs me.

Yes, I have a lot to think about.

I COUNT FIVE WOMEN carrying handmade signs under the large neon logo for Fat Tina's and twelve townsfolk, mostly men, standing close to the highway, just watching. One motorcycle, Angus's Harley, and four vans are in the parking lot: KOM3 and the Joplin *Globe*, the Second Baptist Church, and a familiar white van with no windows, what Sonja calls a "kidnapper van," that belongs to Angus's friend, Sebastian. One more woman crawls out of the church van, complete with her own homemade sign, and two little men barrel out of Sebastian's van.

"A couple of e-e-elephants and we'd have a circus," Sammie says.

"At least the circus eventually leaves town," I say as I park my Hummer next to Sebastian's van.

The two of us sit and look at the scene for a minute. I know by now all these people know what happened last night, and I can't help but think how disrespectful it is for them to be here today, causing more grief.

"Where shall I start," I say under my breath. Sammie looks at me but doesn't say a word. She knows I'm thinking and also knows that it is best not to interrupt.

"I have an idea, Sammie." I open my door and climb from the truck. Sammie is right beside me.

A reporter from KOM3 rushes over, motioning for a cameraman to follow. "What do you think about all this, Fat Tina?" He sticks a microphone in my face. I don't even flinch at being called Fat Tina anymore. It used to bother me, when I was younger, such a cruel nickname, but I am a big woman, and I found a way to capitalize on it. Now, every time I hear it, I think of money.

"It's M-Mrs. Early," Sammie snaps. It bothers her. The reporter gives Sammie a quick glance then turns back to me. I flash my best smile. "Why don't you give me just a minute to chat with these ladies, and I'll be happy to talk to you." I walk tall, straight toward the picketers, never letting the smile leave my face. I motion for Angus to come close, and I lean down and whisper in his ear. As he hurries off, I wink at Sammie and keep walking. She follows me.

Benny Cloud is standing with the picketers, trying to talk to them. They're all screaming at him and shaking their signs, but they go quiet as I walk right in the middle of them.

"Good afternoon, ladies. Any chance I can get you to all go home?"

One woman steps forward, a dumpy woman about my age, her hair going gray at the temples, no makeup, wearing a flowered dress that looks two sizes too big. "We are here until this place is closed for good. God does not condone the type of behavior that goes on behind these doors."

I'm pretty sure I know who this is, but I stick out my hand, manicured nails dripping with jewelry, a stark contrast to her short, unkempt hands. "I'm sorry. I didn't catch your name?"

"Beth Harper," she says, ignoring my hand.

Sammie chokes back a giggle. Daze Harper's wife. I thought so.

I've seen Mrs. Harper a few times but never up close. I can't help but stare, not because she is Daze's wife but because I know that Harley dated her long before she and Daze got married, long before he and I met. I know he had to have seen something in her that isn't exterior, and looking in her eyes, I'm hoping for a glimmer, but I just don't see it.

"Well, Mrs. Harper, I do respect your right to picket my place, even if I don't like the idea. However"—I turn to Benny—"correct me if I'm wrong"—then I turn back to Beth—"I do believe the law says that you cannot stand directly in front of the door. I do believe there is a fifty-foot rule."

Benny chimes in. "Yes, there is. So move your butts fifty feet, or I'm going to arrest every last one of you."

I point toward an area at the north end of the parking lot, where Angus and his friends have started putting up the canvas tent that we use when we have outside events. "As I said, I respect your opinions, even if I don't agree with them. And I don't want to see anyone falling out with heat stroke on my property. So I have some of my men putting up a cover for you, which is about fifty feet away. It will keep you all comfortable and legal."

The women all look at each other then at Benny, who points toward the tent. "I'd say you better take that offer, else I'll have you all sharing a cell by nightfall."

They look at Beth Harper, who nods. Like a gaggle of geese, they walk toward the tent. I stand with Benny and Sammie, and all three of us watch as they make their way across the parking lot.

"What the hell, Tina?" Benny is as dumbfounded as Sammie.

I shrug. "Well, I'm not going to get rid of them, so I might as well use them. I doubt any of those drug dealers are going to be hanging out in my lot with their mommas camped out there. Gives me a little time to figure out what to do about them."

I recognize one of the women—my Mary Kay dealer, Andrea Cranse. She's keeping her head down and trying to stay behind the other women. I wait for her to turn toward me, and I wave. *I see you, Andrea.*

Benny is pointing the rest out and naming names. "See that woman with the white cane, walking next to Beth Harper? That's Billy Jack's grandma."

"She's blind?"

Benny nods. "Went blind about ten years ago. Diabetes."

"Tina, I hate to be the sp-spoiler in all this"—Sammie is talking slowly, trying to get her words out—"but we aren't going to have much business with them here."

"Not from the locals." I motion to the reporter from KOM3. He comes running over, led by his microphone, with a cameraman close behind.

"So, Fat Tina," he says.

Sammie doubles up a fist and makes sure he can see it.

"What do you think about all of this?"

I smile and look directly into the camera. "Protest is the American way, Bob. You did say your name was Bob?"

"No, it's Troy..."

"And isn't freedom of expression exactly what my club stands for?"

"So it doesn't upset you that these women are here?" Troy is fumbling.

"I don't agree with them, of course, but I always say take what you get and try to make the best of it."

"You're not going to try to convince them to leave?"

"I've got a business to run. And by the way, Troy"—I look straight into the camera—"Fat Tina's is having a protest special. Anyone showing an out-of-state ID gets half off the cover as long as these ladies are on the premises."

Fat Tina's sits on the Missouri and Kansas line and within a mile of the Oklahoma state line. The 44 is the crossroads for truckers heading east to west, and north to south. We may lose some local traffic, but the out-of-staters are going to be busting at the doors. And with half off the cover, they'll spend more at the bar and tip the girls a little better. I thank Troy for his free advertisement and turn toward the club.

I don't care who's in my lot. I'm still running this show.

IT'S SEVEN O'CLOCK, an hour before opening time, and I'm already tired. I've decided to stick around until we open, show my face, then go home and spend the evening with Harley and the boys. The church ladies are having their own little show outside, but I figure they won't stick around past ten o'clock.

"What are you thinking about, Sis?" Angus sits at the bar with Sammie, drinking a cherry 7UP.

"Nothing. Everything."

The door opens, letting in the sun, temporarily turning the darkened club into an eye-blinder. Sonja comes in and walks slowly toward the bar, her eyes still adjusting to the darkness. "It sure is hot out there," she says as she sits down next to me and fans herself with a cardboard drink coaster.

Sammie reaches over the bar, grabs a glass and the tap, and gets Sonja an orange soda. I think she's the only one who ever gets orange soda, but I keep it on tap just for her. She takes a big drink and licks her lips. She looks at Angus. "One of your friends is trying to pick up one of the church ladies."

"I wish him luck." They giggle at each other like they have their own secret. I have to smile.

A little over two years ago, Angus showed up at the house with Sonja. He'd been in Tulsa, hanging out with his friends, and here he walks back in with this gorgeous young blonde. Well, "gorgeous" other than the fact that she'd been beaten to a pulp, but I could tell that underneath the black and blue, there was nothing but gorgeous. *"She's a good kid, and she's been beat silly. I couldn't just leave her there,"* he told me.

She didn't talk for almost a month, and when she finally did, after all the bruises and cuts had healed, I realized that the ones on the inside probably never would. We took her to see a doctor in Springfield, and he said it was hard to tell whether her problems came from drug use or just the beatings she'd had. She moved in with Angus in the apartment over his shop, though now that he's got a woman he's serious about, she's planning to move in with Sammie at the cottage. Sonja is like Angus and Sammie's child. Their very sexy twenty-four-year-old child.

Angus is not too keen on her stripping for a living, but he understands that sometimes, you have to use what God gave you to survive. He knows that better than anyone. He saves her money for her and is trying to teach her some other skills that she can use one day soon. She's been apprenticing at his shop for two years now, and he says she's pretty good with a needle.

The door opens again, and this time, Jimmy Ray Wiley walks in. He never did make it out to the club much, always spending most of his time at the jail, and I'm not sure he likes the merchandise I'm selling. Still, he seems like a nice kid. "You all drinking already?" He says it like he's just trying to make conversation.

Angus laughs. "None of us drink alcohol out here, if that's what you mean. Makes you stupid."

"Oh, I didn't mean anything—"

"What's up, Jimmy Ray?" I say. He seems a little embarrassed by his assumption, but he shouldn't be.

"Benny wanted me to come out and check on things a few times this evening. Make sure the ladies out front aren't causing too much trouble."

"What's your poison?" Sammie asks.

"Oh, maybe a water? Thanks."

"Try the orange soda," Sonja says.

Jimmy Ray smiles a big toothy grin. "That does sound good. Okay, an orange soda."

Sammie gets up and goes behind the bar this time to tap him out an orange soda. He takes a big drink and licks his lips, just like Sonja did. "How are you doing, Mrs. Early?" he asks me.

"Fine. How are the ladies out front?"

"Preaching the word. Got themselves a nice little audience too." He turns to Angus, again embarrassed by his choice of words. "Oh, sorry, I didn't mean..."

Angus laughs. "Some of my friends could use a little preaching. And probably some of those church ladies could use some of my little friends."

"Is Benny okay?" Usually it's Benny who checks on us from time to time. I know he has a heart problem and recently found out he's diabetic, so I worry about him. I have a very small circle of people, but Benny is definitely among them.

Jimmy shrugs. "Said he had a lot of paperwork to get done tonight. Trying to take it a little easier now, I guess."

I know Benny has had a hard time recently, given the whole health scare he had, but he sure doesn't seem to be on his game lately. I guess we all have things on our minds these days.

Angus downs his soda and jumps off his barstool. He looks at me and says, "Well, I'm going to go tell Maryanne good night and get back here before we open. You get home to your kids. Don't worry about this place. We got this."

I smile at him, offering him some encouragement. "Let me know if you need me, Angus. You know where I'll be." And I silently say a prayer that Maryanne doesn't ass up on him this weekend.

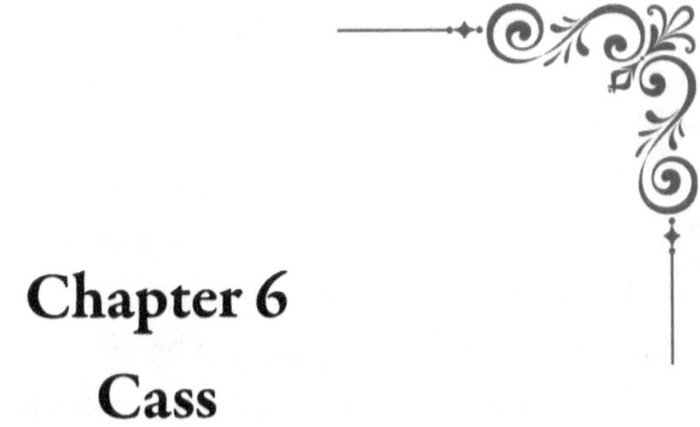

Chapter 6
Cass

After talking to Grams for a little while longer, I came home to take a short nap before Clay returned from work. No matter how much I tried to find a loophole in Grams's theory about not interfering, she basically shut me down. Her logic is that if we try to interfere, we can make it worse, and besides, who are we to try to change what God has decided? I guess I understand what she means about that, but then again, she said our gifts come from God, so why would he give them to us if he didn't mean for us to do something about it? Yeah, I told her that. Yeah, she told me to make my peace. So that means only one thing—I'm going to have to figure out how to keep Maryanne from dying all by myself.

I sleep longer than I intended to and wake up to the smell of something good coming from the kitchen. I lie in bed and take a big whiff—Clay's chili. I sure hope he's making hot dogs with it. I'm in bed looking at the ceiling when he walks in.

He sits on the side of the bed next to me without turning on the lights. "Are you feeling okay, Cassie?"

I let out a long breath. One of the best things about having this baby, other than the fact that I won't have another human being feeding off my body, is that everyone will quit asking me if I'm okay. Besides, it isn't me he should be worried about. I roll over and push him off the bed so I can sit up. "I'm good," I say. But as soon as the words leave my mouth, Peanut kicks me, and I have one of those little contractions that the doctor said are fake. I still don't know how to tell when the real ones come, but he tells me I'll know.

When it stops, Clay is on his knees in front of me, rubbing my legs. "Is it time, Cassie?" he asks. I want to scream NO! But he looks so excited, yet so scared at the same time, and I'm just too tired to get on his ass about acting like I'm going to break.

"I'm fine," I say as I get up and head toward the kitchen, ready for some chili.

Clay dishes it up, and we sit at our little dining room table. He's got some music playing in the background. Country, of course. I take a few bites and have to stop for another fake contraction. Damn, that one came pretty quick.

"Six minutes," Clay says as he looks at the clock. Naturally, he's timing them.

"It's fine," I say as it subsides. I rub my belly and will Peanut to chill out so I can at least finish my chili. "Did Roland ever say anything to you about wanting to go to the beach?"

Clay stops eating and looks at me like I just decided to go streaking through Walmart. Okay, I guess it was out of the blue, but I can't really tell him the truth. He'd only tell me that the visions probably mean nothing. I know better. But in all the years I knew Roland, I don't remember him saying anything about wanting to see the ocean. It didn't seem like the kind of thing he'd want to do, unless there was a really good bar next to it.

Clay puts his spoon down and clears his throat. "Well, uh, no, not that I can remember. When we were little, our dad used to tell us he'd take us to see it sometime, but he left before that ever happened. And I don't remember Roland ever mentioning it. Why?"

I nod. Freddie Adams, Roland and Clay's daddy, left them and their momma when Clay was just five years old, and went off to do his own thing. He's dead too, after Clay refused to give him part of his liver last year. I guess he and Roland are hanging out at the beach now together. It's got to be hell's beach, because I can't imagine either one of them going up instead of down. "Just curious," I say. I can see he's thoroughly confused about me bringing up Roland; we try not to talk too much about him since I killed him last year, so I figure I'll change the subject. "Can I ask you something? If you knew someone was going to die, would you tell them?"

He almost chokes on his chili when I ask this. Okay, maybe I should have stuck with Roland.

"Cassie, I don't—"

I shrug. "It's just a question. I mean, let's say you had a dream about someone dying. You don't know how, or why, or even when, but you think it's real enough that you can't stop thinking about it. Would you tell them?" I just want to know what Clay would do in my situation, without actually telling him what my situation is.

This is one of the many reasons I love Clay. If I'd have said something like that to Roland, he would have laughed at me and called me stupid, but Clay twists his mouth up and scrunches his eyes, like he's really thinking. "No," he finally says.

"Remember when you slid off the road in winter? I dreamed that before it happened," I say. Damn, I never meant to tell him about me seeing things, and now here I am, trying to tell him I'm not really talking about dreams. He knows I have problems, and he knows while I'm pregnant I'm not taking my usual pills, but he doesn't know I see dead people sometimes or that I've been seeing things lately. I guess he doesn't know the really bad stuff. And I don't want him to. I want to take back everything now and just eat my chili, but as usual, I've opened a can and can't really stuff the biscuits back in.

He looks at me for a long time, and I squirm a little in my seat. Then he nods, as if he gets it. "Who did you dream about?"

I put my spoon down, not really wanting any more chili. "Maryanne," I whisper.

He looks at the clock again and gets up and grabs me a throw pillow off the couch just as another contraction hits. When it's over, he's sitting back at the table with his hand over mine. "I'll keep an eye on her for the next few days if it makes you feel better. I'll even tell her why if you'll do something for me."

My eyes are wet not only because the contractions hurt but because he's too good to be mine. "Anything," I say.

"Worry about yourself and the baby. Those contractions are six minutes apart, and they're going to get stronger and closer."

I nod. He's right. Clay's always right.

Chapter 7
Benny

I walk in my bedroom and take my service pistol off my side and lay it on the bedside table. Grace is singing in the bathtub, but I try not to listen because I know she isn't getting the words right. It's late, and I know she's been waiting up for me although she won't say as much. I take off my badge and lay it next to my pistol, unbutton my shirt, and sit on the side of the bed to take off my boots.

Rudy fucking Drown. I can't help but think about what an ass he is. He pretty much ignores Tina's problems, asking only enough to be able to say he isn't totally ignoring his duties but never doing a damn thing to actually help. Sure, he'll send Darnell Dix out there, but I know it's only because he wants to get enough stuff on Tina to shut her down. And nobody from his office ever showed up to get Billy Jack, and I had to listen to him most of the evening, screaming for justice or some shit from downstairs. Then there's the fact that he's sleeping with my mom despite knowing her husband is in prison.

Of course, he isn't doing anything against the law, at least not anything that could be prosecuted as such. But if the county knew about him and my mom, they'd throw him out of office. And if my dad finds out, he'll throw Rudy out a window.

My 1966 Tiny Terry doll looks at me from the corner table, holding that expression that says *What are you going to do about it?* I shrug and give her a look that says *I don't know.* I throw my boots against the wall, and they land on the ground with a loud *thunk.*

"Is that you, Benny?" Grace quits singing long enough to call out to me.

"Was you expecting someone else?" I let out a long breath and stand up a little too fast. My chest hurts like hell, but I won't tell Grace that.

"How are you feeling?"

"Fine," I say. I open the door to the bathroom, and there she is, her hair piled on top of her head and covered up to her nipples in bubbles. I sit on the toilet lid and look at her and just shake my head.

"You look tired," she says. "Have you checked your blood sugar?"

I'm still new to this diabetic thing, and I'm glad that Grace reminds me to poke my finger, but she shouldn't have to. I know when I feel like shit, like right now, it's most likely my sugar's out of whack, but damned if I don't keep forgetting. No, I don't forget. It's more like I'm still in denial about it.

"It's fine," I say, hoping she doesn't realize I'm lying.

"Bullshit," she says.

I let out a long sigh. Like I say, I get the diabetic thing. My mom has been diabetic since I was a kid, and I understand what it means and what you need to do to take care of it. The problem is, I never thought it would be me. I'd gotten into the habit of thinking I was pretty healthy. Not invincible but at least safe. And now, something like this has made me rethink a lot of things.

"Check your blood sugar. Then get some sleep." She has one of those big poofy pink sponges, and she rubs her neck, then down one arm. On any other day, the sight of her in the tub like that would get me excited, but tonight, I'm feeling more like a steer than a bull.

"What's that smell?" When Grace takes a bath, the room is usually like a field of wildflowers, but tonight, it smells more like burnt wood.

She holds up a small silver ball that was floating in the tub with her. "Something new to hopefully help with my sleep problem."

"You mean nightmares. Damn, Grace, I thought those went away?" Grace has dreams sometimes that she won't tell me anything about, but I know they scare her because when she wakes up, she goes in the other room to read. That's always been Grace's way of taking her mind off something she doesn't want it wrapped around. I hate that she won't talk to me about it either, but that's kind of her way, too.

"They aren't all nightmares. They're just... weird. Anyway, I'm seeing someone that might be able to help me with it," she says.

"By having you stink up the bathroom with a little silver ball?" I ask.

She smiles. I love that smile. "It's a diffuser ball. Aromatherapy. And it doesn't smell that bad."

"I'm ready to get things back to normal around here," I say.

"Normal?"

"Yeah. We can start with you sleeping through the night. Jimmy's going to be leaving for KLETC soon, Harvey's getting that new patrol car the city promised, and with Tenesy getting out of prison next month—"

Grace lies back in the tub and plays with the bubbles on her chest. "We have a new normal, Benny." Damn if that woman doesn't always know what I'm thinking.

"Yeah." I grab the little testing kit on the bathroom sink, load a clean needle in the gun, and poke my middle finger. Damn, I forgot to get the machine ready first. I start over, gun loaded again, strip in the machine until it says *ready*, poke, blood on the strip, and wait. "Seventy-three," I say.

"Too low before bedtime," Grace says matter-of-factly.

Something has been really weighing on me, and if there is anyone I can talk to about it, it's Grace. But I haven't been able to bring myself to say it. But I need to get it off my chest. I take a deep breath. "You know, for a year, I made the election one of my top priorities. I wanted to be sheriff, for a lot of reasons, but now…" I stop and run my hand through my hair. "I'm glad I didn't win."

There, I said it.

"Oh." She stops playing with the bubbles and reaches into the water and pulls the plug. She stands up, half her body still covered in bubbles, and wraps herself in the towel that's hanging on the rack. I wanted to be sheriff most of all so I could do better by Grace, give her all the things she ever wanted, because she deserves everything. But the truth is, I like my job. I like being able to be with her as much as I can, and if I were sheriff, I don't think that I'd get to see her as much. This diabetes scare has made me look at things a lot differently too. I just want to be happy and have a long life with the woman I love. I just hope that's enough for her.

She steps out of the tub and sits on my lap, putting her arms around my neck loosely. The towel dislodges and falls around her, but she doesn't reach for it. With one hand, she starts rubbing my head. It sure feels good.

"Do you know why I love you?" she asks. I think that's an odd response to what I just told her, but you never know with Grace. "It's because you are a good man. I know not everyone in town sees it, but deep down, you are a good and a just man."

I put my arm around her waist. "I just like things how they are, Grace. I don't want you to think I was scared." *Or less than a man.* I can't say that.

"I know. But sometimes, things change, and…" She kisses me on the chin and adds, "We'll be fine."

That's exactly what I needed to hear. I start to tell her that when the phone rings. It has to be the station, and it has to be something important or they sure as hell wouldn't be calling. Grace gets up and grabs her towel, and I go to get the phone but not before tapping her on the ass. I may not be in the mood, but my wife looks good naked.

It's Angus. I put it on speaker and sit the phone on the kitchen counter while I dig in the fridge for a bedtime snack.

"Chief, I hate to bother you. But you said you wanted to know when the protestors packed it up for the night at Tina's. They just left."

I look at the digital clock on the stove—9:46. "I hope it's a one-night thing," I say. Those ladies must be crazy.

"They seem to be focused. They plan to start about noon tomorrow, according to Beth Harper," he says.

I decide I'd just as soon have a peanut butter sandwich, so I shut the fridge and head to the cupboard instead.

"You still there, Chief?"

"Yeah, yeah. Okay, well, I'll see if I can get Daze to talk to his wife tomorrow. I don't like them out there. Tina has enough problems." And so do I.

"All right. I'll see you in the morning, then. It's going to be a long day, Chief."

I take a bite out of my sandwich and can't help but think how much better it would taste if Grace had made it. I swallow and then answer. "Always a long day," I say.

Chapter 8
Maryanne

After I send repeated texts to Shaylene all morning, she finally answers during my morning recess. *Made it home. Taking a nap. See you after school.* I resist texting back to ask why she hasn't answered any of my previous messages, but I'm sure she would give me some lecture about it not being safe to text and drive and say that she told me she'd be home by ten o'clock. One day, she'll have kids of her own, and she'll understand. When Mom sends a message, you pull over and answer. Period. But she's going to be here all summer, and I don't want to get off to a bad start.

I don't have playground duty, but I'm not too keen on sitting in the teachers' lounge. It's nothing but a gossip pit, and I don't want to be a part of it. I'm sure without me there, they have more to talk about, anyway. So I'm sitting in my classroom, checking messages and making calls. I have a lot to get organized in the next few months, and it seems the more I try, the more goes on my list.

I've been wanting to go back to school for years, work on my master's degree and try to move up a bit. It's not that I don't love my job, I do, and teaching sixth grade is probably the best grade anyone can teach. The kids aren't too young, but they aren't in middle school yet, either, so they don't think they're little adults. They still like their teachers, for the most part, and my kids have always seemed to like me. When Roland was alive, work was a lifesaver for me, and I didn't even realize it. He'd come over in the mornings for coffee, and I felt so empty when he'd leave. Then I'd go to school and have a room full of eleven-year-olds who liked me, who needed me. I'm going to miss that.

But with Shaylene off at college, Roland dead, and my relationship with Angus getting stronger every day, it's time for me to grow too. I'm excited about school—terrified because I'm going to feel old, but very excited. I'll substitute during the next two years, but it won't be the same. I have no idea what's down the road for me, but it's definitely time to see.

My phone dings, and it's a message from Angus. *Did Shaylene make it in yet?* I smile. He's been worried about her, too, this morning, but instead of saying so, he's been telling me not to worry. He's not her daddy, but he already acts like it. That's one of the many things I adore about him; he has his "people"—Tina, Harlan, Sonja, Sammie, Cass—I can't really call them just friends, because once you become one of his, you're more like his family. Shaylene and I are now part of that odd mix, but he also makes sure I know I'm at the top of the pile.

I text him back. He's at the shop today and said he needed to work at Tina's this evening, which will give Shaylene and me time to be alone and talk. I wipe the little beads of sweat from my lip just thinking about it. *Stupid.* Stupid of me to think my daughter wouldn't understand. During Christmas break, she got to know Angus and told me several times how much she liked him. When she calls during the week, she always asks about him, and it's sincere. Why I am so worried about telling her that I'm moving in with him is beyond me. Maybe it's me that's worried about it, and I'm just projecting it onto her? I shake my head. No, I'm sure about this.

I think.

The problem is that what Cass said yesterday is right. I was stupid for cheating on him when he went back to visit his family, and if I really want this to work, I have to be up front with him. And I do want it to work.

I think.

I let out a deep sigh. What I haven't told anyone is that after Roland died, and before Angus and I started seeing each other, I had considered leaving Deacon for good and starting over someplace else. After all, everything that came out after his death about our relationship didn't do much for my reputation in town, and I just felt like without him, and with Shaylene off at college, this wasn't the place for me anymore. I sent out résumés to all of the places that I thought would be fun to live, places with a beach, and I was excited, really excited about the possibility of moving.

Then I met Angus, and that all changed. He made me feel special again, so I put the idea of leaving away and decided I'd go back to school, another of my dreams, instead. And last week, I got accepted for the master's program, and I thought, yes, I'm making the right decision. But the very next day, I got a call from the San Diego school district. And now I'm not so sure.

I decide I better check on Cass before the kids come running back in for social studies and math. *Wednesday Adams*. It wouldn't surprise me if she did name her kid that.

She answers on the first ring. "Save me," she says.

I just laugh. I know Babe Shatner, Cass's grandmother, is on Cass detail today until Clay gets home, and that means she's pampering her like a sick kid. It drives Cass nuts, and that's a short drive. "She won't even let me take Dog out to pee by myself. I guess she's afraid I'm going to drop Peanut out by the worm huts and forget to bring him in."

She tells me that her back hurts really bad this morning, but she isn't going to tell Babe because she's afraid she'll make her drink some nasty potion. "And she has my fridge stocked with crap. She says there's a bad storm coming, and she wants to make sure we're prepared."

I glance toward the window. It's gray and cloudy. Even someone without Babe Shatner's sight could have called that one. "Are you still having contractions?"

Cass called me last night before she went to bed, which was unusual, but I'm glad she did. I can almost hear her roll her eyes through the phone. "Yes, but they're still not any worse than they were. Did you tell Angus what a cheating scumbag you really are?"

I roll my eyes right back at her. "It's not that easy," I say. I'm worried. I know that he's the best guy I've ever met, and I know he loves me, and I love him too. But what I did was so stupid. He'll be mad and hurt, but I think he'll get over it, and we can move on. It's that mad-and-hurt part that's going to be so damn hard. "And besides, with Shaylene here this week, I—"

Cass's cackling cuts me off in the middle of my thought. "Oh, yeah, right. Use Shaylene as an excuse. You need to tell him tonight. He's got a big surprise for you this week, and he needs to know about your extracurricular activities before he..."

"Before he what?"

"Just do it," she says and hangs up the phone.

My class is starting to pile in the door, and one of the Sweeton boys smiles and points at the phone in my hand. "Talkin' to your boyfriend?"

I ignore his question and put my phone in my purse in my bottom desk drawer. That doesn't keep him from starting the chant that his buddies are happy to join in with. "Miss Spencer and Mr. King, sittin' in a tree, k-i-s-s-i-n-g. First comes love, then comes marriage, then comes—"

"Stop!" I put my hand up and speak just a little too loudly but enough that they shut up real quick.

Then comes marriage.

Oh no. Please, Angus, don't let that be the surprise.

Chapter 9
Benny

I got this little game out at the Cracker Barrel last week. It's a triangle with holes drilled in it and a golf tee for each hole except one. The object is to jump tees, remove the ones you jump over, and try to get all the damn tees off the board except one. Grace did it on the second try; I've been working on it for a week, and the best I can do is three. I'm currently at five, and I'm sitting at my desk, trying to analyze what my best next move will be, when Jimmy comes in my office carrying a Chihuahua. I put the game back in my drawer and cross my hands on top of my desk. "That must be Schmegel."

Jimmy shakes his head. "No, this is Taco. I've been looking for Schmegel since yesterday, and Mrs. Meadows said she let Taco out to see if he could find Schmegel, but then he never came back either. I found this little guy under a dumpster behind the post office." He sets him on my desk, and I run my hand in front of his face. He doesn't flinch.

"Is Taco blind?"

"Blind as a bad date. I called Mrs. Meadows. She's coming here to pick him up."

He's sniffing around my desk, and I figure the little guy is hungry. I open my drawer and pull out one of the low-carb protein bars that Grace sends with me every day. She thinks I eat them for a snack, but they taste like cardboard, so I give them to the prisoners when they start asking for extra food. I break off a few pieces and put them in front of Taco. He won't eat them either.

"She's real upset because it looks like it's going to storm real bad, and the extra humidity just makes Schmegel's breathing worse and—"

I hold up my hand to stop him. "Tell her we're doing what we can. And to stop sending blind dogs out to find him." I grab the remote control on my desk and turn on the weather report. On a clear day, the map is solid green. Today, it's covered with slashes of yellow and red, from Texas to Illinois.

"Anything else going on I need to know about?" It's been a slow morning, which is a good thing. I've got R.T. downstairs waiting for his wife to get off work so she can come bail him out, and Billy Jack, still there, waiting for the sheriff to send someone over since yesterday. I swear, Rudy does this shit just to piss me off.

Jimmy's mouth is hanging half open, and I feel like shoving one of Grace's protein bars in it. "Well, in case you haven't noticed, there's a big storm heading this way," he says.

I cross my arms over my chest, nod toward the TV, and stare at him. "Other than that."

"Nope, just a lost dog. I'll go search around the library and down by the park. How far can a Chihuahua travel in a day?"

I shrug. Pretty damn far, I guess. "Hey, Jimmy. I want to talk to you real quick. About KLETC. I know you're going to do good, and I just want you to know..." Damn, I'm not good at this sappy stuff. The truth is, Jimmy is young, and he's a good cop, and I know he wants to move up. But I like him here. It's hard to find someone that you can trust and that you can work with, and well, Jimmy is my guy.

"I know, Chief. I'm not going anywhere. I got friends here." He gets a big goofy smile on his face. I recognize that smile. I used to put it on every time Grace walked into my hospital room at the VA. Damn, Jimmy's got a boyfriend. And I didn't even know it.

"Well, just so you know, I—" The door to the station opens, and I wait to see who's going to appear in my doorway. It's Levi Dinger. And it's about time. "I thought I asked you to be here yesterday?"

Levi stutters around a little bit like a schoolkid. "It was my mom. She was real sick, and it was my birthday, and…" Wendie Dinger is dying of cancer and, from what I hear, ain't got many days left. I gotta give the kid a pass on that one. I motion for him to sit down in the plastic chair across from me. Jimmy waves from the door.

"What were you doing at the club Sunday night?" I ask him. Levi's a pretty good kid, and I've never had a problem with him, so I figure I'll go easy on him. But I still want to know what he saw at the club.

"It was my birthday. Well, at midnight. I was waiting in the parking lot until midnight so I could go in. I didn't see anything, though."

I shake my head. I'm not that stupid. "Yeah, you did. Just tell me. Rocky's going to give me the details sooner or later, and you don't want me coming to you later and calling you on a lie. Not good, Levi."

He's thinking. It doesn't take him long. "Okay, I saw Billy Jack out there, but I didn't talk to him or anything. Then I saw Rocky go back to where he was, and then I saw Billy Jack pull out. But Rocky never came back, so I went out there and found him and ran to get one of them guys in a pink shirt. That's all I saw. Really." He says it so fast I have to replay it in my mind for a minute.

"So you didn't actually see Billy and Rocky fighting?"

"No. I didn't see anything. Just that. Honest."

I nod then look up at the TV and the big round clock next to it. Straight-up noon. "Why aren't you in school?"

He smiles. "It's senior skip day."

And you come to the police station. I'm just about to tell him how dumb that is when my phone rings. I pick it up while Levi reaches for Taco and starts talking to him like a little baby. It's Tina.

"Beth Harper and her gang are here again, and we're closed on Tuesdays!" she says.

"It's gonna rain. I'm sure they'll leave then," I say. Surely even Beth and the ladies are smart enough to come out of the rain.

"They brought umbrellas. Look, I need you to come talk to them. I'm only here for the beer delivery, and I don't like people being on the property while I'm not here. I told them that, too, but they seem to think they're above trespassing."

"I can't leave right now, but I'll give Daze a call. Not sure if it'll help any. Just do what you're there to do and leave their asses in the rain." I slam the phone down. Damn, I was down to five pegs in my game, and Beth Harper has to start her shit early.

"Everything okay?" Levi pets Taco, and the dog curls up on his big lap, ready for a nap. I look up at the Weather Channel running on the TV. Harvey's on patrol, Jimmy's out looking for an asthmatic Chihuahua, and Tina wants me to tackle the church ladies. But I got two prisoners downstairs, and if I don't get them their lunch in the next thirty minutes, they'll be screaming that I'm trying to starve them, then I can look forward to more paperwork when they file a complaint. I look at the TV: red slashes coming up through Tulsa and a few scattered twisters reported down. A bar scrolls across the bottom of the screen, saying a tornado watch is in effect until five o'clock in several counties. Cherokee is included. Damn.

The thing with tornadoes is this: In Southeast Kansas, we get hundreds of sightings every year. Most of them blow over or never touch down, and some of those that do hit ground do it out in the middle of a field, so the damage is minimal. They're mostly wind, not tearing shit down. Those of us who grew up in the area just get kind of used to it; it's part of our weather, and we don't always mind too much about it. But all it takes is for one to land in the wrong spot, and a place turns to hell real quick. We witnessed that firsthand a few years ago when an F-5 went straight through Joplin. I ain't never seen anything like it. Hit the hospital where Grace worked, and I thank everything holy she wasn't there that day.

"Levi, can I trust you to do me a big favor?" I ask. "Sit here and hold Taco until Mrs. Meadows gets here. And watch the TV. I want to make sure that storm coming our way is nothing but lightning and rain."

"Well, yeah, but you're just going to leave me here? What if something happens?" Levi is bigger than most men, but I have to remember, he's still a teenager.

I stand and clip my radio on my belt. "I'm not leaving you. I have to feed our guests real quick. Fifteen minutes. If anything happens, yell downstairs."

I go to the back to microwave some crap that is approved nutritious and delicious for the prisoners and put it in the little compartmentalized Styrofoam trays. I radio the fire department while I'm playing waitress, and get Bucky Crow.

Bucky has been the fire chief for ten years, and he's an okay guy. Runs a clean department, spends a lot of time and money on training, and has access to two dozen volunteers if he needs them. The city council bitches about the cost of his department about every other meeting, but I support him every chance I get. They won't bitch about the cost if Deacon ever needs them. We don't have a lot of fires in Deacon, at least no more than any other small town. But a lot of people don't realize all the things the fire department does. It's a lot more than fires. And in Deacon, Bucky is the guy who blows those big sirens when a tornado is close enough that everyone needs to take shelter.

Bucky has already put his volunteer force on alert and says he's just waiting for the call from the national weather forecasting folks at the Advanced Weather Interactive Processing System to hit the button if need be. I don't know why all of a sudden I'm feeling a little queasy about this storm more than any other we've had recently. But I am. I say a little prayer, like I always do, that Deacon has a fire department that is on their toes. I make a note to put my auxiliary on alert as soon as I get up to my office, and I head downstairs.

When Billy Jack sees me coming, he starts screaming about his rights, like he knows what they are. I ignore him and hand him his tray through the slot.

R.T. shakes his head. "Damn, if I'd of known I was going to have to share my basement with that little ass, I'd of saved that twelve-pack for the weekend."

I hand him his tray. I don't like R.T. He's a wife beater, and if his wife would just leave his ass and quit bailing him out, we'd get rid of him for good. But knowing the mouth on Billy, I can't help but feel a little sorry for R.T.

For just a second or two. Yeah. Then it's gone.

When I get upstairs, I expect to walk in and find Levi and a Chihuahua, but that ain't who's sitting in my chair with his feet propped on the desk.

It's my dad, Tenesy Cloud.

"That kid said he had to go get his girlfriend," he tells me. "They're letting the high school out early 'cause of the storm. I told him I'd watch TV for ya."

When Tenesy got sentenced to prison, he was hauled off right out of the courtroom, in the suit and tie my mom had bought for him just for that occasion. I saw him in it once, the day they put the cuffs on him and led him out, and I remember thinking what a scene that was—he looked good, all slicked up. Except for the steel bracelets holding his hands behind his back.

When they let him out this morning, they gave him the same clothes he went in with—that dark-blue suit with a red-and-blue pin-stripe tie. The suit's now three sizes too big and a few years out of date, so instead of looking like a middle-aged businessman, he looks old and homeless. I should be sad, in some way, about how he looks, but he's sitting behind my desk, and my pissed off-ness about that overshadows any sadness.

"Get your feet off my desk and get out of my chair," I say.

He gives me that little Elvis-wannabe sneer that I hate but does move. Slowly. "Nice to see you, too, asshole."

He grabs one of the straight-backed chairs from the wall and turns it around backward and straddles it. When I was a kid, I thought that looked cool and couldn't wait until my legs were long enough to do that. Now it just makes him look more like a thug than he is.

I look around for Taco but don't see him. "Where's the dog?"

"Bottom drawer. Little fucker tried to bite me." I open my bottom drawer, and there sits Taco, shaking. I pull him out and put him on my lap, and he immediately pees. *Damn.* Tenesy hasn't been back five minutes, and I'm already tempted to strangle him.

"Where's Mom?" I ask.

He sucks his teeth. Another little habit I hate. "She don't know I'm here yet. Thought I'd surprise her."

Great. Hopefully, he'll surprise her while it's still daylight, because if he shows up there after bedtime, he might be the one surprised. "How'd you get here, then?" I glance up at the TV, and that big red slash is getting closer to Deacon.

"They handed me a Greyhound ticket, and it seemed like a crime to waste it. Thought I'd stop here first, see the man in action." He turns his head all around, like he's looking for something. "Is there one around here?" He snickers at his own joke and sounds like Dick Dastardly's dog, Muttley. Another thing I hate.

I look at the TV. Another tornado's reported down, this one about fifty miles down the interstate. We've got a pretty good chance of seeing one today, and I can only hope that it's a small one and we see it from a distance. And I hope it passes soon, because the first thing I intend to do as soon as it's safe is call my mom and have her come get Tenesy out of my office.

But right now, I've got a problem. With Jimmy gone, I can't just leave an ex-con manning the police station with two people locked up below and a terrified blind Chihuahua pawing his way around my desk. And regardless of what Tenesy has to say, I've got work to do.

I call Daze Harper and tell him to go talk to the churchwomen, then I call the auxiliary phone tree to get some extra help on the streets. Heavy rain and wind alone are enough to double my workload today, and I want to be prepared.

Tenesy walks around my office, touching everything while I'm on the phone, like a kid with no manners. My head's starting to hurt, so I grab one of those nasty little bars that Grace sent to work with me, then have second thoughts and throw it back into the desk. Bucky Crow walks in just as I hang up from my third call and glances only briefly at Tenesy before pointing at the TV.

"I called the school board and told them to send everyone home early. It's about to get real nasty out there, and we have to keep people safe. Don't need any more work to do than we have to."

Tenesy laughs from the other side of the office. "Shit, it don't look like you all do much, anyway."

Bucky ignores him and continues to look at me. I like Bucky more each day.

"Thanks, Bucky. How long before we're out of the danger zone here?"

"An hour or two. Mother Nature is a little pissed today, but if we're lucky, those storms will keep going, and we'll write this off as a training day." He pauses for a minute. "You want me to give County a call?"

He and I both know that's my call to make, and I appreciate him volunteering, but dammit, I have no intention of running from Rudy Drown. "I got it, Bucky. Thanks."

I pick up the phone and start to dial, and Tenesy is at my desk with his hand on the cradle before I can hit the speed dial. "Don't tell him I'm here." His eyes are wild, and I can't tell if he's scared or desperate.

I slap his hand away from the phone. "Sit down and shut up before I lock your ass up myself."

He gives me that evil glare but does as he's told.

I'm not afraid of Rudy, but I'm also not a glutton for punishment, so I change my mind about calling the county office and dial Darnell Dix direct. He answers on the first ring. He doesn't even ask why I'm calling him instead of Rudy's office, but he says they've been watching the storm and they've got everyone on alert, just in case the worst happens.

Then I grab my cell phone and walk outside to call my mom. She doesn't answer, and so I call Grace instead. She's at work, and I know if she's busy, she'll have to call me back when she sees my message, but I need her advice about my dad right now, and lucky for me, she answers on the first ring. "Hello, handsome," she says.

I look back to make sure Tenesy didn't follow me. He didn't, but he's a sneaky ass, so I keep my voice down, anyway. "I got a problem," I say.

"Well, maybe I can make it better." I can tell she's smiling by the way her voice is a little higher than usual, and I'm glad she's having fun today, because I sure as hell ain't.

"Tenesy showed up in my office, got out early, and wants to 'surprise' Mom. I tried to call her, but she didn't answer. I don't want to be the one to tell him, but I don't want him to show up this evening when Rudy is getting comfortable, if you know what I mean."

I hear her let out a little air and suddenly feel bad for deflating her good mood. "Well, you can't tell him."

"No shit," I say.

"I'll keep trying to call your mom, and you keep him busy. And don't worry about it too much. I need you in a good mood tonight." She's smiling again. I swear, I think I even hear her giggle.

"What's going on tonight?" I say.

"I got a little something special planned."

"Oh, really." That usually means she's fixing a fancy meal and wants to watch a movie on the TV. I sure hope she isn't cooking anything too spicy. I've been chomping on Rolaids for heartburn the entire morning as it is.

"Seven o'clock. Not a minute past. Don't be late," she says.

I head back into the station just as Grace says "I love you," and I say it back.

As I hang up, I look at Taco then my dad then at the TV. My first thought is, *How can things get worse?* But I live in Southeast Kansas. It can get a lot worse. Very quickly.

Chapter 10
Tina

When I got home from the club last night, Harley had already put the boys to bed, saying they both had a head cold. He had a blanket in one hand and a picnic basket of goodies in the other. He was serious about us spending the evening together on the dock by the river. I had been a little anxious about taking a break from the club, but in truth, I'd missed those times with Harley. Not everyone is as lucky as I am to have such a man, and I need to find more time to be with him. We watched the river flow by and reminisced, talked about the boys, and eventually, talked about the club and our future.

"I've made a good run of the club," I said. And I have. Regardless of the problems we have in the lot, or the disdain from the sheriff, or the protestors, or anything else, men keep coming. It is a moneymaker and would be for anyone. "I could sell it for a small fortune and do something else."

"True. But if doing something else is all this is about, you could keep the club, let Sammie run it, and open another business for yourself," he pointed out. "After all, you've built that business up. It'd be a shame to see it continue making money and you not getting any of it."

He's right. That's really the biggest issue for me: the money. It's not that we need it. We've got enough to retire right now if we wanted to, and there are days when that sounds wonderful. But if I had to dig deep into myself, I'd say I was a business junkie. I love the high of making a buck, and I'm damn good at it.

"And besides," Harley continues, "if you opened something else, something 'reputable,' it'd just fail, and everyone in town would have the last laugh."

"What? That's not true! How can you say that?" Harley has never been anything but supportive, and for him to say something so cruel—

He winks at me. "That's what you're thinking, isn't it?"

Oh, Harley, you know me so well. I tell myself I don't have to prove anything to anyone, but that's not true. I grew up in this town, always called names, being treated like I was lesser than everyone else, and it gives me great satisfaction to flash my money in town. If I were to fail...

"But I won't fail," I say.

He pats my leg. "That's my girl. You do what you want, but I think you can do it all."

I hug him so close, I think I might break him. "I love you, Harley. But reverse psychology? Really?"

He shrugs. "I think Dr. Phil called it 'confronting your inner saboteur.'"

I have to laugh. "Well, you aren't very good at it."

"We'll see."

We eventually made our way back to the house, made love like we did a decade ago, and fell asleep in each other's arms. It was wonderful.

Then the morning came. The boys were both sick, and the cool breeze from last night had turned into a gray morning.

Life goes on.

Even though the club is closed on Tuesdays, I still have responsibilities. The cleaning crew comes early in the morning and basically sanitizes the place. I usually go in about ten to inspect it, work on any pending issues, and balance the books. By two o'clock, our beer delivery shows up, and by three, our hard liquor order arrives. I inventory everything and am usually done by four. Tuesdays are typically my one evening a week at home.

I'm drinking my coffee on the back porch when Sammie comes in, followed by Sonja.

"It looks pretty n-n-nasty out there," Sammie says.

I glance outside, and the wind is whipping through the trees. "Yeah. If it starts getting worse, I think I'll just go in for the deliveries this afternoon and save the paperwork for later."

"Sonja and I can handle the deliveries. Stay home," Sammie says.

"Yes! I like the beer guy," Sonja adds.

"Bruce," Harley says as he walks on the patio. "The 'beer guy' is Bruce, and he just called and said he's going to be early because of the weather. They're projecting a big one by late this afternoon, and he wants to get done and get home."

"I probably should call about the liquor," I say.

"Already did. He said don't wait for him. If he ain't there, he'll get you tomorrow before opening. Sammie's right, she and Sonja can handle the beer. Or I'll go. You need a break. Might as well take it today."

"I wonder if the protestors will be there today." I don't really wonder; I'm sure they will. I guess I just wonder how long they'll stay if the weather gets bad.

Harley hands me a sheet of paper. "Just in case, I pulled up a release and sent it to your computer. They need to sign those, anyway, if they're going to be on the lot."

I look it over and smile. Harley always seems to have my back.

"Thank you, but I'll go. It shouldn't take more than an hour, and since I wasn't there last night—"

Harley shakes his head and winks at me over his coffee cup. "You're a control freak, that's your problem."

I smile. "Yeah, yeah. And you need to stop watching Dr. Phil."

I get to the club about twelve thirty, and of course, Beth Harper and her crew are waiting. A few of Angus's friends from last night are there, too, and although I'm not paying them to be here, I'm glad they are. Keep the ladies out of trouble, so to speak.

I don't even wave but go straight into the club, turn on the TV over the bar, and call Benny. We live in Kansas, for God's sake, and it's tornado season. I swear, those women must live on something other than common sense.

After Benny assures me that he'll call Daze, I go to my office and pull up the release form that Harley sent me, make a few corrections that I didn't want to mention to him, and print off several copies. There's a knock at the door, and after I let Bruce in, we watch the weather on TV for a few minutes. It's bad. And heading our way.

"We can reschedule, Bruce," I say.

"No, I'm here, and it shouldn't take me more than thirty to forty-five minutes. We got time," he says.

I sigh. Yes. We've always got time.

When I go outside armed with my release forms, Daze Harper is there with his wife, Beth. They've moved out from under the cover I provided for the ladies, closer to the club, apparently so they can talk in private. Well, talking isn't exactly what they're doing; arguing is more like it, from the looks of it. If it weren't for the storm coming and me wanting to get home, I'd call Benny and have him come get her for violating the fifty-feet distance she's supposed to keep from the club. That would teach her, and I'm sure the rest of her crew would pack up quickly with their leader gone. But I haven't got time for that right now. My only concern is to get them off my lot or, if they won't leave, at least make sure I'm relieved of any responsibility for them.

Beth sees me coming and hushes Daze. Like I care to listen to their conversation. I'm pretty sure I know how it goes. He's trying to rough-talk her into leaving, and she gets more hardheaded with every word that leaves his mouth. I can't imagine how their life at home must be. I walk right past them toward the canopy, more concerned with what's going on in the sky.

About a dozen women and three of Angus's friends from Tulsa are under the canopy. I know the men feel some sort of responsibility to stay as long as the women are here, but they aren't employees of mine, just friends of a friend who have volunteered to help keep things under control while I try to work this thing out. I have no intention of them getting hurt in the process. I look at the men first and tell them to take down the canopy and get out of here as quickly as they can.

I don't say another word to the women until Daze and Beth have joined us. I knew they would follow, being too curious to stand away and miss what I'm going to say. "Ladies, I have no problem with you being here," I say. "None at all. I respect you for standing up for what you believe in, even if we disagree."

Nobody says anything. They all just stand there, waiting for me to continue.

"However, I've been watching the news, and there's a storm heading our way. A big one. I've got the men taking down the canopy before it blows away, and I'm concerned for your safety. So I'm asking you to go home and get out of the weather before it gets really bad."

Beth walks slowly toward me as if challenging me. I'd love to wipe that smugness off her face.

"God will protect us. We're happy to sit in our vans until the rain lets up." About half of the women nod in agreement, but the other half are whispering among themselves.

I believe in God's protection, but I think one of the ways he provides that is by giving us the ability to reason and thereby protect ourselves. Beth seems to think it means something else. I shake my head and hand Beth the papers I printed off my computer. "I had a feeling you'd say something like that. Fine. If you're going to be out here, I'd appreciate it if you would sign these waivers, stating I warned you about the dangers and you chose to stay of your own accord." I point at the beer delivery truck behind me. "As soon as my delivery is complete, however, I'm leaving and taking cover, so you'll be on your own."

Beth grabs the papers from me and signs her name on one without even reading it. She hands the rest to the other ladies, and after some discussion, a handful walk to their vans and drive off, while another handful sign their names, pass the papers to me, then cross their arms across their chests.

I turn and head to the club. I'm not going to try to convince grown women to do what is obviously in their best interest. If they want to be stubborn to try to prove a point, let them. But I'm planning on riding this storm out in the safety of my storm shelter at home.

Daze catches up with me about twenty feet from the club. "I tried, Tina," he says.

"It's real serious, Daze. There's tornadoes touching down all over, and I'm hoping they'll see the light soon. But I'm not staying around. They're on their own."

Daze points at Bruce, who is hauling cases of beer through the front door so fast that I'm afraid he might topple his hand truck. "How long before he's done?"

"About thirty minutes." I hand him one of the release forms. "I'm sorry, but if you're going to be out here, I need you to sign this too. I'm not going to be responsible if something happens."

He hands it right back without hesitation. "Nope, don't need one. I got me a twelve-pack of PBR and a nice, big safe room under my tool-shed in the garage that will ride out any storm. If Beth don't want to crawl in it, that's more room for me and the kid."

I look at the sky again and the ominous bank of clouds that seem to be getting darker by the minute. "Hopefully, it's just another spring storm, and we'll be back to normal by this evening." It's starting to drizzle, and I look at Daze one more time. "Take care of yourself."

"You too," he says. Then he heads to the lot, and I turn back to the club.

THE BAR AT FAT TINA'S extends twenty feet across the back wall. Behind it is a mirror with shelves four high that Sammie keeps stocked with just about every kind of liquor. She keeps the bar polished to a high shine. The bar is lined with stools, the kind with spindled backs that swivel all the way around so the customers can order from Sammie then turn around and watch the show. At the far end of the bar is my chair, a custom version of the standard bar set, but six inches higher, with a cushioned seat and back and three times the width. I'm usually moving around the back of the bar, but when I do sit down, I can see the entire operation from my perch. That's what Sammie calls it, which is appropriate. I'm sitting on my perch, listening to the rain and wind hit the building outside, waiting for Bruce to finish unloading the beer into the cooler and watching the weather map on TV. It doesn't look good.

My phone rings—Harley's third call in an hour. "He's almost done," I say when I pick up the phone.

"It's coming up fast," he says. "And there's tornadoes to worry about—"

"I'm watching, but it's just a warning right now. There's not one down."

"Are those women still out front?" he asks.

"Yes, they're still out there," I say.

"Fine. You get out of there as soon as you can. I love you," he says.

"I love you too."

Bruce comes in, pushing a dolly of beer cases. "This is the last load, Tina." Bruce has been our delivery guy for several years. He's always on time and doesn't mess around, just gets his job done and gets on his way. Now he wheels the dolly into the cooler and stacks the cases on top of the rest, leaving enough room down the middle to walk and grab what you want. Sammie likes it organized, and Bruce knows exactly how she likes it kept. "That storm is right on us. I'm going to have to pull the truck around to the side and wait it out for a bit. It's moving fast, so shouldn't be too long."

I take a deep breath. I had a feeling that was going to happen.

"Go pull your truck around and come back in. I'm going to wait it out, too, now. No use in putting myself in danger."

He smiles and looks relieved. Only someone half crazy would want to wait outside in this kind of weather, and I've got two vans of crazy people out there right now. I call Harley back to let him know. He's not thrilled by the idea but knows I'm safer inside than driving around, even if I do have a heavy vehicle.

I get off my perch and head toward the door. The bar phone rings, but I don't answer it. The sky is completely gray—that big black cloud looks to be right over the Downstream, less than a mile away. It's pouring rain, and there's only one van left in the lot. At least Angus's friends had the good sense to leave. Bruce comes back holding an umbrella. We stand there and look at the van together. "Let's go," I say.

He doesn't seem any more anxious than I am to make one last effort to get those ladies out of the storm, but at least we can say we tried. Some people don't have sense enough to come out of the rain. Literally.

Bruce holds the umbrella, and I try to get partially under it with him, but it isn't doing any good. I knock on the window, and the woman in the passenger seat rolls it down. Her eyes are big as baseballs.

"Honestly, ladies, this has gone too far. You need to come in the bar and wait this out."

They start chatting among themselves, and I'm starting to get angry. I'm standing here, getting wet, and I'm not too happy about it.

It's Beth Harper who speaks. "We appreciate the offer, but—"

"Tina!" Bruce screams so loud even Beth Harper shuts up and turns to look where he's pointing. The big black cloud over the Downstream is funneling down fast.

"Let's go!" I turn and start running as fast as I can toward the club. Behind me, I hear the women hurling themselves out of the van. Bruce and the ladies pass me before we get to the door. I glance back and see it's almost to the ground before I slam the door and lock it. As if a few dead bolts are any match for a tornado.

"Shut the cooler off," I say to Bruce. He knows exactly what I'm saying and is on it before I can get past the ladies, who are standing around gawking like it's the first time they've ever been in a bar. "Move it!" I scream at them and point toward the cooler in the back. They move. It may be their first time in a gentlemen's club, but it's not their first tornado.

Bruce starts to move out some of the cases he'd just put in. I stop him. There's no time. I can hear shingles blowing off the roof. I direct the ladies single file up the middle of the cases of beer, and they waste no time complying. There are six of them, and as the front door of the club blows open, I know it's on us. I also know that squeezing Bruce in with the ladies is going to be all the room there is. There's no way there will be room for half of me, much less the entire package. I push him up the middle and shut the cooler and throw the latch.

Then I'm all alone, looking around the club I've called my second home for over a decade, wondering what the hell I'm going to do now. The only sound is the wind and the rain, and as the first part of the roof blows, I know this is it. I look around one more time. It's too late. I have nowhere to go.

Bottles are falling off the shelves behind the bar, glass is smashing, and I turn away, not wanting to see. I look at the stage and the pole and—

The pole.

"God bless you, Harley," I whisper as I rush to the back of the stage, get on my hands and knees, and rip the utility panel off just as half my roof disappears above me. I don't look. I crawl under and get on my stomach and start army crawling over wires and cables, toward the pole.

When we built the club, Harley wanted to be in charge of picking the pole that the dancers would use when they do their routines. I thought at the time that was a pretty strange thing for someone to be so focused on, but I let him be in charge of that. It was like a big secret to him, and the day they had it installed, he wouldn't even let me come down until it was secured. "There it is," he had said. I had shrugged. It just looked like a pole to me.

I can see that big smile on Harley's face when he pointed at the pole, so proud that day. "Check it out."

I ran my hand up and down the pole. "It's great," I said.

"No, wrap around it. Give me a show," he said.

I was only about four hundred pounds at the time, but I knew there was no way. "Harley..."

"It'll hold you. I had them reinforce it to a thousand pounds. They had to drill down five feet to secure it, but that pole ain't never going anywhere."

"Harley, I can't," I said.

He put his arms around me and kissed me. "That's all right, Tina. One day, you're going to wrap around that pole for me. I know you got it in you."

I'm crawling beneath the stage now. I hear the mirrors above the stage crash overhead and resist the urge to stop. My fingers brush the pole as the stage falls on top of me. I push with everything I have and hook my elbow around it then pull my entire body, and what's left of the stage, with me.

Then I wrap my body around that pole and hold on.

For Harley.

Chapter 11
Cass

Grams is trying to rearrange my refrigerator so she can fit more crap in it, and I'm standing behind her, wishing my back would stop hurting so bad. It's been throbbing all morning, and I feel real sick to my stomach, and I'm wondering if Peanut feels sick too. I rub my belly and feel him move a little bit. My belly seems to have a mind of its own and squeezes him like it's trying to tell him it's okay.

"When the baby gets here, you need one shelf just for baby stuff. Then when you get up in the middle of the night, it'll be right here, and you won't have to dig around." She turns and looks at me then stands up real quick. "Are you okay?"

Busted. She already knows I've been having false contractions all night and all morning, but I didn't want to tell her about my back because she'll have me soaking in a tub and lying in my bed for the rest of the day, and I just want to clean my house. Not that I can bend over too far to do that, but I want to be doing something other than lying around waiting for something to happen.

I give her my best fake smile, which isn't very good. "I'm fine. I probably shouldn't have eaten those other two chili dogs for breakfast." The thought of the hot dogs dripping with cheese, chili, and onions makes me hungry, and my mouth waters. Then my stomach squeezes a little, telling me not to fill it with any more crap.

"Maybe you should sit down." She pulls a chair from the little dinette we have in the kitchen and holds my elbow like I can't sit by myself.

"I'm good, really." I walk to the back door and look at the sky. The rain has settled on a slight drizzle, and I want to go outside. There's a big, dark cloud in the distance, and it doesn't look like it's producing much rain, but you never know. "I need to take Dog outside while the rain has slowed down some. He doesn't like to pee in the rain."

She grabs her raincoat off the dining room chair and wraps it around me. Then she grabs her umbrella. "Let's go." Dog looks from me to her like he's waiting for his rain gear too. I reach down as far as I can, and he jumps up on my leg. "Sorry, fella, you have to tough it out." He sniffs my belly a few times and lets out a low whimper then sits down at my feet.

Dog and I had a little talk this morning. Well, I did most of the talking, and he just nodded like he knew what I was saying. We were lying in bed, Dog curled up next to my stomach like he usually is, and I was trying to explain to him that when Peanut gets here, I'm still going to love him just the same. They say it's important to make older brothers and sisters know that when a baby comes they're still loved. Since Peanut doesn't have any older brothers or sisters, I figure Dog is the closest he's going to get. But Dog understands. The way he sleeps next to my belly, keeping Peanut warm, I think Dog figures I'm having a puppy. After our talk, he hasn't been farther than two feet away from me all day. He's taking the big brother thing pretty serious.

My phone rings. It's Lola. She had planned on coming down today but said she's running late and will be leaving Springfield about five, after her husband, Richard, gets home from some meeting he's at. Richard is retired, but he has more meetings than a banker, and I figure it's not a meeting at all. He's probably at the country club, hobnobbing with the other old guys who have nothing else to do but talk about how great they were when they were young. Or maybe they show each other dirty pictures of their trophy wives. Clay went with him a few times, but he said he was sworn to secrecy about what the guys did at "the club." He winked when he said it, like it's no big deal, anyway. I don't really care. As long as Richard's good to my sister, I won't hit him upside the head with a shovel.

I put the phone on the table and turn to the back door again. That cloud is still miles away, but it's getting bigger and moving in this direction. I like storms, I love the rain, but I like them better when I can run around and stomp in the puddles, not when I'm wrapped in plastic and trying to keep my belly from squeezing me silly. Grams is still doting around, so I try to take her mind off of me and point at the cloud.

"You were right, Grams. Looks like a big one heading our way. What do you think, it's out by the Downstream about now?" I figure the idea that her prediction of a big storm coming true will make her happy, but when she turns and looks at the big black cloud in the distance, she grabs the back of the chair and looks like she's about to fall down. This time, I grab *her* elbow and move her to the front of the chair, where she plops down, accidentally popping the umbrella open that she has in her hand. That can't be good, but she doesn't seem to notice, just keeps looking at the cloud. I move the umbrella away and get in front of her, but she looks around me, out the back door, watching the cloud. "What's wrong?"

She points at it, and I turn to look again. Yep, getting bigger and definitely coming this way. She picks up my phone and starts punching numbers. "Clay, where are you?"

I know where Clay is. Shaylene got in this morning, and Clay wanted to spend some time alone with her this afternoon. He knew Grams would be with me, so he took off at noon and has been sitting at Maryanne's house with Shaylene since, waiting for Maryanne to get out of school. Clay's being a daddy, which he's so good at. So yes, I know where Clay is, and so does Grams, but she asked, anyway.

"Is Maryanne with you?" She shuts her eyes and slowly shakes her head, and I know that means that yes, she must be there.

"Do not leave there, you hear me? I don't care what it takes, you and Maryanne and Shaylene stay in that house." Now she's starting to spook me. I don't know what she sees in that big black cloud, but I feel a rock in my stomach when she says that, and with everything else going on in there right now, a rock is not something I need.

"Clay, I know you don't always believe what I see, but you have to listen. Do not get in your truck and drive right now. Stay put. Cass and I are fine. Just fine." She pauses for a second, probably because she's spooked him too. "Look out the back window. See that big cloud?" She's pointing again, and I turn to look, knowing Clay and I are both looking at the same thing from different sides of town. "Keep looking," she says. "And... there."

Grams has freaked me out a lot in my life. Like when she told me one time not to eat the Whoppers from my Halloween bag, even though they are one of my favorites, then the next day, there was a big deal about how someone had put poison in their Whoppers and passed them out to little kids. She's also been wrong, though, like when she kept saying I didn't really kill Roland, but I did. But I'm looking out the back door, and just as she says "There," a funnel drops slowly from that big black cloud, all the way to the ground, and it's almost as wide as the cloud itself.

I grab the phone from her and hear Clay on the other end saying, "I'm coming home."

"No!" I say. "Do what Grams says. I mean it. If she says we'll be fine, we'll be fine. And if she says you stay put, you stay right where you are." He tries to argue, and I watch the funnel get bigger and bigger, and it's moving toward town. We hear the sirens go off in Deacon, and that means take cover. "Clay, I love you. But stay put. Please." Then the phone goes dead. Of course.

"Grams?" I don't like that she mentioned Maryanne. Clay promised to keep an eye on her for me, but the way Grams told him not to move... I bang the phone on the table a few times and try to call Clay back. No, no, no. If this is Maryanne's time, and Clay tries to stop it...

Grams has her eyes shut, like she's praying, which probably isn't a bad idea. Dog is doing a little howl from the sound of the sirens and pees on the linoleum. I grab some paper towels and throw them on it and squat down in front of Grams the best I can and hold on to her knees. Her forehead is all scrunched up, like she's about to cry. "Grams, talk to me. What did you see?"

She pats my hand and smiles down at me. It's fake as hell and is so twisted it almost looks like it hurts. "We're going to be okay," she says.

"But what about Clay?" *And Maryanne. And Shaylene.* Dog is next to me, whining. Grams wipes her eyes.

"We're going to be okay. We don't have time to get into town to a shelter, but the bathroom will serve us just fine. Let's focus on us right now." I don't like the sound of that at all. Grams stands and grabs my hand, and we make our way through our bedroom to the bathroom, grabbing the blankets and pillows off the bed on our way.

"Close those shutters," Grams says as she points at our small bathroom window. I'm watching that big black cloud move closer to town, and all I can think about is Clay. I try to think real hard, hoping he can hear me, and tell him to please stay put like Grams said. I feel my eyes fill up, and just when I'm trying to fight back my own tears, it feels like an invisible rubber band about a foot wide wraps around my lower belly and snaps shut, squeezing with everything it has. I fall forward, my head on the windowsill, and scream at the top of my lungs, just as Dog lets out a howl that would make his wolf ancestors proud.

"Don't hold your breath!" Grams rushes to my side. "Oh dear, not the best time for you to go into labor!"

Labor? That's what this is? I've heard a lot of women say it's the most painful thing they have ever gone through, and I thought they were probably just not that tough. But I am tough, and if what I'm feeling right now is the start of it, I'd say all those women tended to downplay the pain. I stay at the window until the pain slows down some, and she helps me stand up.

That big rubber band squeezes me again, and I scream until I can't scream any more. Grams tells me to squat, and she helps me down. When it's over, she helps me back up. "I've got to run in the kitchen and get a few things. I'm going to lay some of the blankets on the floor," she says, "and then I'll check you. After the storm passes, we'll hightail it out of here. We just have to wait this out a bit."

I turn to the window and throw the shutters closed, as if they'll keep the storm out of this bathroom, and make my way to the pallet that Grams has made on our linoleum floor. She returns from the kitchen holding a bowl.

"Grams, I peed myself."

She looks down and smiles. "Your water broke, honey. You're about to be a momma."

I'm crying again. I can't stop. *It can't happen this fast.* "I need to get to the hospital." *But my phone isn't working. And there's a tornado out my window.*

She holds my face in her hands and forces me to look at her. "There's no way we can get through this storm. If we have to do this here, that's exactly what we're going to do. Do you hear me?"

"I'm scared." And the tears flow. This isn't the way I expected it to happen.

"Don't you be scared, honey. I've been watching videos on how to do this for months now, just in case. I can do this. And you can too." Great, my Grandma Midwife learned how to deliver a baby on YouTube.

I start laughing, and Grams probably thinks I'm crazier than I am, but she keeps guiding me to my position on the floor, and I try to get myself situated. The clock in the kitchen screeches twice to tell me it's two o'clock, the sirens from town are blowing in the background, Dog has joined in with his own little medley, and I know behind me, that big black funnel is heading our way. And I'm about to have a baby.

Of course I am.

It couldn't happen any other way.

Chapter 12
Clay

Shaylene got in this morning while I was still at work, and I watched the clock like a kid at Christmas, waiting for noon. Maryanne won't be off work until three, and Babe is hanging out with Cass today, so for three hours, Shaylene is all mine. I like that, me and my girl, hanging out, doing nothing but being together.

We thought about running over to Joplin to the batting cages—I hate to think my soon-to- be-nineteen-year-old daughter can out-hit me, but I've watched her play, and I figure she probably can. The weather changed our minds on that one, though. Nobody likes to be out much in a storm, especially one as big as the TV says this is.

Instead, we decide to hang out in front of Maryanne's TV and eat all her food. She's got her fridge stocked, and I know it's because Shaylene is home for the summer.

"Mom's making a big deal out of having a boyfriend," Shaylene says as she dips a chip in the big bowl of ranch dressing that we found hidden in the crisper drawer. "I mean, so what. Good for her. She doesn't need my approval, you know."

"Your mom has always needed someone's approval. Now that you're an adult, I guess that duty falls to you." I'm not trying to be mean and talk about the girl's momma, and I say it with as much niceness as I can, but it's true, and Shaylene knows it.

"Well, maybe if she keeps seeing Angus, she can deflect some of that on him." She takes a big drink of her Dr Pepper and makes a face. "I haven't drunk soda in a long time. It's kind of nasty." She sits it back on the coffee table and grabs more chips. "Anyway, I like Angus, and I think it's great that she's moving in with him. She's been happier in the past few months than I have ever seen her in my life."

"She told you she was moving in with him? I thought she was keeping that for tonight."

Shaylene smiles. "You always fall for that trick, you know that? I'll try to act surprised. But what's the big deal? She's so..."

I nod. She doesn't have to finish the sentence. Whatever that word is that describes Maryanne slips my mind a lot too.

Shaylene puts one of her legs under her and is sitting on it in kind of a cross-legged way on the couch. It looks uncomfortable. "So tell me about my little sister. What are you going to name her?"

"You mean your little brother? We haven't picked names yet."

A lot of people think it's kind of weird that we haven't really talked much about baby names. I mean, he's close, and we probably should have something to call him. We went through a lot of names, but it just wasn't working out much for us, so we decided we'd rather see him, then we both think we'll just know. It keeps us from going through baby name books every night or being on the internet. I'm fine with waiting.

"Oh, a lot of my friends do that, too. It's cool."

It's raining hard, and a big thunderclap hits and spooks us both.

"Your friends? You're not even nineteen. What friends of yours are having kids at nineteen?" But I know Shaylene won't do that soon. She's too focused on school. And on her sports. I want Shaylene to have plenty of time to enjoy her life. Kids can come later. The last thing I want is her rushing into anything.

"My friends that aren't lesbians."

Oh, yeah, there's that too. I'm still not used to the idea that Shaylene likes women instead of men. It's not that I think there's anything wrong with that—it's just who she is. But I'm still an old country boy who grew up believing that there's a certain way to do things. You grow up, you fall in love, you get married, you have babies, and the rest just works itself out.

The thing is, I can't honestly say that old way has worked out too well for everyone I know. Maryanne had a baby and never got married. Cass got married but killed her husband and is now having *my* baby. So maybe it isn't about following the same outline for everybody. As long as you can be happy, maybe following your own plan is the way to go. And like I say, I'm okay with Shaylene doing what she needs to do to be happy. I'm just not used to hearing it, that's all.

I hear the front door open, and I glance at my watch. Ten till two. "What are you doing home so early?" I ask as Maryanne breezes into the house like she owns the place. Well, she does, but this was supposed to be my time with Shaylene.

"Have you looked outside? They let school out early," she says.

My phone rings, and I look at the number: Cass. Just seeing her name light up on my little phone screen makes me smile, and I figure it's going to do that for a long time. She's due to have a baby in two weeks, which I know really means any day. Our baby.

It's been hard for me to accept that too. Oh, I can't wait to have the little guy, have him sit on my lap and steer the truck, teach him how to play ball, show him how to be a good man. But I'm forty, and less than a year ago, I was living alone, getting my family where I could. A big difference a year makes. I've got Cass, and Dog, I've got a half brother, Britt, I never knew about until a few months ago, and there's Lola and Richard and Babe Shatner, and of course, Shaylene and her goofy mother. I think the word is "overwhelmed." I'm overwhelmed by my blessings and just hope God doesn't think he's given me too much too quick.

I answer the phone, and it's Babe, not Cass. "What's wrong? Where's Cass?" Shaylene is switching channels and settles on the weather channel. Actually, I don't think it's *the* Weather Channel, but I think the weather has gotten so bad that all of the channels are technically the weather channel right now. Big red marks dot the green map, showing tornadoes dropping out of the sky all through the Midwest. It's going to be one of those days. I hate those days.

Babe tells me to go to the back door, and I do. Shaylene follows me. I can see a monster cloud, somewhere out by the highway. It's difficult to tell, but definitely too close to Deacon for my liking. "Yeah, I see it. It looks like a bad one."

Babe pauses for a second or two then says, "There." Just as she says the word, a big funnel drops from the cloud like she'd done it on demand.

"Oh crap," Shaylene says beside me. *Oh crap* is right.

"I'm on my way," I say and start to put down the phone. But Babe tells me not to leave, to stay put. I don't want to stay put. I want to grab Shaylene and Maryanne, jump in my truck, and get to Cass as quickly as possible. Not that I think I'm any match for a cloud like that if it decides to hit, but I want to be with the people I love most if something happens. I don't mean to sound morbid, but I'd rather die with them than live without them.

But now Cass is on the phone and tells me stay put, and I'm going to trust that. She tells me that they'll be all right, and I'm going to trust that too. Seems like a lot of trust, I know, but when a woman can trace a cloud and pull a tornado out of it, you tend to listen to what else she has to say. I glance at Maryanne and see that she's put her coat on and picked up her purse, and I shake my head. I promised Cass last night I'd keep an eye on her, and maybe this is the time I'm supposed to do it.

I hang up the phone when the alarms downtown start blowing. Even from here, we can see the funnel is on the ground and heading toward our little town. I put my arm around Shaylene. "It's going to be okay," I say.

"Come on." She grabs my arm and pulls me toward the front door. "Archie's Store is a shelter, and that's just three blocks away. This one is too big to wait it out, Daddy."

I stop her. "Shaylene, Babe Shatner said we'll be fine right here and said we need to stay put. I know she's a bit nutty, but..."

Maryanne rolls her eyes. "If we need cobbler, we can call Babe Shatner." She points out the back window. "That thing isn't cobbler, and she isn't a weatherman."

"Please, three blocks and we're safe," Shaylene adds.

They're already heading toward the door, and I don't think taking the time to argue with them is a smart thing to do right now. They definitely win on the logic side, but I'm still not totally sure logic is the only way to make a decision. And they're right—it *is* just three blocks. We've got time to get three blocks. And I'm damn sure not letting them go alone.

"Let's go," I say.

Chapter 13
Benny

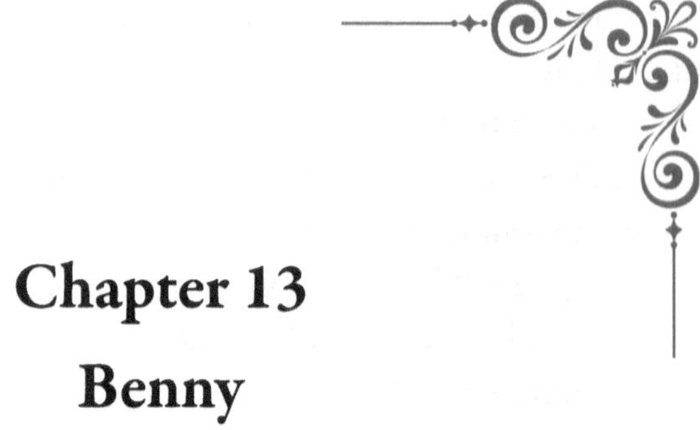

It's almost two o'clock, and just as I start to wonder where Jimmy is, I hear him walk in the door. He's talking to someone, and as they get to the door of my office, I see it's Mrs. Meadows, come to claim Taco. He barks when he hears her voice, and she picks him up from my desk and kisses him like a baby.

"Oh, you good little boy! Went out to find your brother, did you? Don't you worry, we'll find Schmegel." She sniffs back some tears, and Taco licks her face. "You sweet thing."

I look at my wet pants. *Sweet* ain't exactly the word I'd use.

"I am so sorry I haven't found Schmegel," Jimmy says. "I promise, I'll start looking again just as soon as this storm is over."

Something about an old lady crying has to just melt a heart like Jimmy's.

I hear the door blow open, and papers start to fly all around the office. I get up, but Jimmy is at the door before me. We stand there together and see a big black cloud, somewhere out by the Downstream.

"That looks wicked," Jimmy says.

"Mrs. Meadows, I think you and Taco need to get comfortable here for a little bit until this cloud blows over. We don't want to be out looking for the both of you later." As much as I'd like Taco to leave, I do have a responsibility to keep the citizens of Deacon safe, and sending Mrs. Meadows out in this storm doesn't seem like the way to do that.

"You oughta do what he says," Tenesy yells from my office. "This TV says that big red thing is heading right for us."

Mrs. Meadows turns toward the TV. "Oh my."

Jimmy and I keep looking at the cloud. "'Oh my' is right. Jimmy, see if you can get Tina on the phone, and make sure Daze took care of all those women out there."

Tenesy mumbles something to Mrs. Meadows, and she giggles. I don't even want to know. I keep looking at the cloud while Jimmy calls Tina at the club. "No answer," he says, returning to the door with me. There's something hypnotizing about that cloud, like a swirl of black, gray, and white, moving as one large mass. The rain has slowed some, and so has the wind, and if I were home right now, I'd love to be curled up in bed with Grace, listening to the storm outside. Nothing better. Nothing better than Grace, period, but add a good storm to—

"Chief." Jimmy doesn't scream, and he doesn't whisper either, but something in his voice makes me chill and pulls me back from my memories.

My eyes follow in the direction he's pointing. "Of all things holy..." I'm a faithful man. I believe in God, and I know from past experience that angels are real. But I think that when most of us think about how powerful our God is, we tend to think of the good things he's capable of, and we often forget about the things that don't usually work out too well for us humans. I can't explain why he does it, but once in a while, he shows us that no matter how hard we try, there are some things that we as mere mortals are incapable of controlling. As I watch that funnel drop straight down out of that monster cloud, I know this is one of those times.

The sirens go off, and I know Bucky has been watching too. I say a quick prayer then take a deep breath. Time to go to work.

"Damn, Ruben, you didn't have to go to all this trouble to welcome me home." Tenesy has snuck up behind me. I don't have time for his shit.

"Get downstairs. Take Mrs. Meadows with you." I look outside, and as soon as those sirens started blowing, people from the post office across the street and anyone in the businesses downtown that are close enough to make the walk are heading toward the station.

"Bullshit, I just got out of jail." Tenesy walks back into my office. I'm glad to let him ride it out up here.

"Jimmy, get Mrs. Meadows down there. I'm going to send these other folks as they come in, so post yourself down there and direct traffic." I count at least twenty heading our way right now, and I'm thinking my two-cell basement is going to be packed full by the time that cloud gets here. I hold the front door open for them as they make it inside, and tell them to head downstairs, while looking back toward the monster heading our way. It's the biggest I've ever seen, has to be a mile long, and it's touching ground. If the direction is off a bit, it'll hit out by the old bridge, out by Clay Adams's house, and I'm hoping he ain't home. But if it comes right through town…

Angus is running down the street toward the station. It doesn't surprise me he's the first to show up, and I gotta say, I'm thankful as all get out for that. He's a little out of breath and stumbling for words, which surprises me.

"Benny." He stands at the top of the stairs, looking at me, not losing his focus as people pass between us. He's scared, and I guess he's earned that in his life.

He doesn't talk about what happened that day the Twin Towers fell, but Tina told me. He was late for work one day and stood outside and watched the second plane hit the second building. He was right there, in a thousand-dollar three-piece-suit, when the first one fell. He woke up, covered in dust, in the front seat of a fire truck. Never did find out who carried him to it and put him there. He brushed himself off and did what he could do to help that day, calling his roommate until his phone went dead. He waited for him to show up back at their apartment, but he never came.

Angus showed up in Deacon not long after that. Learned how to do tattoos and opened his shop. He feels like there were a lot of people on that day who made sure some nobody little guy made it home that night. And in return, he does what he can to help others. That's why he's on my auxiliary force, paying back something that he can't even name.

"Angus, I need you right now." I'm trying to be understanding about his fear, but I do need the guy.

He nods his head and clears his throat. "I just talked to Harlan. Tina and all those women are at the club. And it's right on them. He can't even get up the road yet."

Damn. There's nothing I can say.

Angus takes a deep breath and straightens up to his full four foot, six inches. "Where do you need me?"

I pat him on the back, the equivalent of a man's hug, and he smiles. "Get downstairs and take over for Jimmy. Send him up here to get some supplies just in case, and I'll man the door." He doesn't hesitate, and I know he'll be an accommodating host to the townsfolk who are going to be our guests through this. He may have a few cracks in him, but he's as solid as any man I've known.

"He's standing here acting like he runs something," I hear Tenesy say behind me. He's on the phone. He sticks it out to me, and I realize it's my cell phone. "It's Grace," he says.

"Where did you get my phone?"

"I took it out of your pocket when you weren't paying no attention, Deputy Dog."

I can hear Grace calling my name through the phone. "Get downstairs," I say to him.

"I done told you, I ain't—"

I grab a handful of his oversized suit in my hand and pull his face so close I could kiss him. "There's only one person in charge here today, and that's me. Now get your ass down those stairs, or I'll throw you down them." I push him in the direction of the open basement door. He sneers at me once then obeys.

"Grace," I say. I can barely hear her over the sirens. She's in Joplin and rounding up a group to head to Deacon just as soon as the storm passes. She knows the damage that a storm like this can cause. She also knows that I need to know she's safe. "Stay put," I tell her.

The radio on my hip squawks. It's Harvey Cox. "Chief, it's coming over the bridge, right up the middle of town. Oh, Jesus, Benny, I can't—"

"Harvey, get out of there, now. You hear me? Harvey?" There isn't any response, and as much as I want to throw the radio, I put it back on my belt. I'm going to need it today.

"Benny?" It's Grace again, so I put the phone up to my ear. "Grace, it's here. I gotta go." I tell her I love her, and I mean it. She says the same, and I know she means it too.

"Benny," she says before she hangs up. "There's only so much you can do. A hero is one thing, but don't try to be a superhero. Be safe."

I check on things downstairs. Jimmy has R.T. and Billy Jack hauling water, and I think, *Good job, Jimmy. Put those boys to work doing some community service.* Jimmy follows me back upstairs for a final check. There ain't nobody else on the street, and the door blows out of my hand, wide open. Jimmy comes over to help me pull it to.

"This is it, Jimmy. We got about five minutes. Let's get downstairs." We're pulling the door shut, and suddenly Jimmy stops pulling.

"Wait," he says and runs out the door and down the front steps at full speed. The wind is whipping in every direction, and I run after him, screaming after him, but he can't hear me. I can barely hear myself. I have to grab on to the flagpole to keep from being blown away, and I know I've made a big mistake. There's no way I can get back up those stairs and into the building. I think about Grace. *Stay safe*, she said.

I'm so sorry, Grace.

I look across the street and see Jimmy, trying to make his way back across the street, holding a Chihuahua. Schmegel!

Our eyes meet, and he smiles.

Then he's lifted off the ground and flies off like a superhero.

Chapter 14
Cass

When I was a kid, one of the big events of the year was watching *The Wizard of Oz* when it came on one of the three channels we got on TV. Grams would make a big tub of popcorn, some homemade candy, and Coke floats with peppermint ice cream. Then she, Grandpa Jack, Lola, and I would camp out in the living room and watch as Dorothy went from Kansas to a magical world of witches and talking scarecrows. We knew all the songs, and Lola and I would stand up and do the parts we knew best, acting it out like we were the Lollipop Guild or the Lullaby League. Lola's favorite character was Dorothy, naturally, because she was pretty and had nice shoes. Mine was the Wicked Witch and her flying monkeys.

Lying on the bathroom floor, in between the contractions, I'm focused on the window. The shutters are swinging slowly back and forth because I didn't secure them well, and the wind outside is blowing so hard I keep waiting to see Almira Gulch ride by on her bicycle with Dog in the basket. I know that when the room stops spinning, I'll be in Munchkinland, needing to find my way back to Kansas.

I'm thinking about how I'll do things differently than Dorothy did when another wave of pain starts, and I scream for Grams. She grabs my hand and forces me to get up.

"Come on, honey. You know the position." Grams is convinced that the best way to have this baby is to squat, which isn't the easiest thing to do when you're heavy in the middle and the middle feels like it's about to explode. She grabs the little step stool I keep in the bathroom and pushes me down so that I'm sitting on the edge of it, my face at the lip of the bathtub, and gets behind me to hold me in position. I lay my forearms on the tub and rest my head on them and turn to look out the window. A worm hut flies by. Clay is going to be pissed.

Dorothy was too nice. She picked up every straggler along the way, and although they might have helped her a little bit, I think she'd have done better if she just took off down that road by herself. If one of those Munchkins were as smart as Angus, I'd take one of them with me. And Dog would be there too. He'd probably pee on the Yellow Brick Road.

I scream with all I've got, but it's hard with the storm going on outside. Grams is panting behind me, and Dog is beside me, panting just like Grams. I try to follow their lead, but all that comes out is another scream. I want to push. I want to push with everything I have to get this child out of me, to make the pain stop.

"Don't push," Grams says in my ear.

Of course not. If I could stomp my foot, I would, but I don't have the energy to do anything but squat. The pain releases a bit, and I fall back into Grams's arms, hoping she can hold me but not really caring if I fall on the floor. Her arms are around me like she'll never let me go. I hear a loud crash in the living room and feel the wind coming under the bathroom door. "I think the windows just blew out," she says. She hoists me up and puts me back on the floor as she goes to secure the shutters on the bathroom window. I get one more look before she does. Hay... an oilcan... flying monkeys...

"Dog," I say, just as another wave of pain rips through me. Grams has the stool behind me, and I grab the side of the bathtub and hoist myself back up on it. Without the window, I try to rely on my childhood memory. Me and Lola, with her singing "If I Only Had a Brain" and me singing "If I Only Had a Heart," but all I can see are the flying monkeys, stomping on Scarecrow, ripping his insides out. I want to push.

"Don't push," Grams says.

The pain lets up, but I know it won't be for long. Grams puts Dog in the bathtub so I'll have something to focus on during my next contraction, and I'm thinking how confused he must be to see Grams yelling at me to squat instead of him.

"Clay," I moan. "I want Clay." This isn't how it was supposed to be. Clay was supposed to be with me, and we were supposed to be in a hospital in Joplin with a doctor, not in my bathroom with Grams and Dog. I know if Clay were here, he'd wrap those big arms around me and push Peanut out for me. But he isn't. I feel like I'm at the Emerald City only to find out the Wizard isn't real.

"Clay's going to be fine. I told him to stay put. If he tried to leave, he wouldn't be fine. We can do this." Grams has her fingers between my legs, and I don't care. When she's done feeling my privates, she pats my leg. "I can feel the head. It's almost time."

I start crying, and Dog looks over the bathtub at me. "I changed my mind. I don't know what to do with a baby. Grams, I can't do this."

"Oh, we're doing this, all right." It sounds like an explosion goes off in the house, and Grams ducks, even though there's nothing flying around in the bathroom. The pain is back, and Grams helps me get in position, but this time, she puts my back against the wall and gets in front of me. I put my hands on her shoulders for support.

"Don't push," she says. "Breathe."

I see Auntie Em in the giant crystal ball, calling for me. I can't hold back my tears. *Auntie Em, I'm frightened.*

I feel my entire body split up the middle, and I scream so loud that Dog howls.

"Don't push," Grams yells.

I scream louder, and something releases below me.

"Push!" Grams yells, and I push so hard I feel the veins in my head popping out, and I feel something else popping out too. Then the pain stops. And all I hear is the wind rushing through my house and Dog whimpering in the bathtub.

Grams is pulling things out of her little bowl—shoestrings, craft scissors—and I crawl to my bed on the floor. I don't want to look. I don't hear anything.

Then I hear a cry. A baby's cry.

I look up, and Grams is wiping a tiny body and face with a big fluffy towel, then she wraps it in another so only the face and arms are sticking out and puts it in my arms. I put a finger out, and the baby wraps an entire small hand around it and holds on.

"He's so red, and hairy, and... Grams, is everything... okay?" I can't quit looking at that tiny face, and suddenly, a feeling goes through me that I don't recognize. This is mine, something that Clay and I created, and I feel something in my heart that I've never, ever felt before. Grams is crying, and it's been a long time since I've seen her do that, but she's also smiling.

"Perfect. In every way. She is perfect in every way," Grams says.

I feel something else come out of me and think I'm having another baby, but Grams takes care of whatever it is and puts it in her bowl. Then she lies down next to me on the floor and wraps her arms around me and my baby.

"Hello, Stormy Em." I look at Grams, and she nods. "This here is Grams, and that's Dog. And I'm your momma." Stormy is quiet, and I think she's listening to me, and I intend to tell her everything I know. The wind is starting to die down. It sounds like a train that has already left the station. "And all that noise out there? That's a tornado. Welcome to Kansas."

No place like home.

Chapter 15
Tina

I've always been considered a strong person, not just physically but mentally. For the record, though, while being at least twice the size of everyone else your age for as long as you can remember has a way of making your skin thicker, that doesn't necessarily translate to toughness. Most people like me aren't stronger than anyone else. In fact, many are so haunted by the negative reactions from others that they are often depressed, sensitive, and deeply affected by their weight issues. In other words, we aren't stronger; we've just had a lot of experience building up walls and a facade against the rest of the world, so we appear tough.

But the truth is, size is not an indicator of our strength. That comes from within. As I lie under the stage, holding on to the stripper pole with all of my physical strength, listening to my club fall around me, I cry. Not for the loss of the business—I have good insurance if I want to rebuild—but because I am alone, scared, and I don't want to die.

It all happened so fast. It couldn't have been more than five minutes. There were tremendous crashing sounds, like a jet airplane was landing next to me. Several times, I felt pressure as chunks of wall and ceiling crashed on the stage above me, only to be swept quickly away by the winds. I thought of letting go of the pole a few times, ready to accept whatever fate was mine, but I kept a mental picture of Harley and my boys in my head, and the thought of leaving them made me hold on, even when I felt like my arms were about to be pulled from their sockets. I held on. And the pole stayed with me.

Finally, I can tell the tornado has passed. I hear the wind whipping above me, and I know it's raining; I can hear the drops on the stage overhead. I try to move, but I'm trapped. The stage that has fallen on my back has protected me but is also holding me prisoner. All I can do is wait and see.

My body is holding the stage up, so I have a two-foot view of what's before me, but I can't move. Daylight is just outside my grasp, so I know the building is gone. I'm outside and am watching the rain fall into puddles in what was once my parking lot. I keep hold of my pole, as if letting go will result in my giving up, and I refuse to give up now. The worst is over, and as far as I know, I made it through. I'm alive. Unless I'm dreaming.

The thought frightens me, and again, I start to cry. What if I didn't make it? What if my mind is tricking me, another defense mechanism, and I'm actually dead or near dead? I cannot move, and I feel no pain. *Possibly dead*, I think, and my wails become louder.

"Tina!" I hear Harley, but it's muffled and in the distance, like I'm at the end of a tunnel and he's standing in the light.

"Harley," I try to scream, but my throat is dry, and I barely make a sound. I try to move, just a little, but I can't. I keep looking at that one sliver of daylight, and I see boots. I feel the cold steel of the pole I'm holding on to, and I remember where I am. I'm not dead. I'm stuck, the stage is on top of me, and it won't budge. But I'm alive, and there are boots, right there. I lick my lips and try to muster as much spit as I can, but my words still come out as just a whisper. I want to cry again, but I want to be found. I need to make noise, and I can't. It's just me and the pole.

And the four carats of diamonds I wear on my fingers.

I flip my rings around so they're facing my palms, and I begin to slap the pole. The first ding is faint, so I slap harder. I can hear it over the wind, *ding*, and I start beating the pole with everything I have. I shut my eyes and focus all of my energy on beating that pole. *Ding, ding, ding!*

Then I feel the weight being lifted off of me, and I feel the first drops of mist. I open my eyes and see Bruce and all the church ladies and Sammie and Norm Dinger, all lifting the stage off of me. And Harley. "Harley," I whisper.

"We gotta get you out of here, Tina. They can't hold that stage up forever." He unwraps my hands from the pole. "Do you hurt?"

I shake my head. I'm sore, but I don't hurt. I move my legs and my arms; they work. I sit up then roll over to my hands and knees and crawl from under the stage, with Harley by my side. Once we're clear, I lie on my back and look up at the gray sky and start laughing.

My dress is ripped in several places, and I have cuts and bruises all over my arms and legs, but they work. Harley is checking me out, and I'm in the middle of a circle of people, some looking at me, others looking in the direction of Deacon, most crying.

"The boys?" I ask.

"They're fine. Sonja is with them. It didn't even rock the house."

Slowly, I get up and make a useless attempt to brush the mess from my clothes and body and look toward Deacon. The tornado is easily a mile wide and is going straight through town. I stand with the others and watch, knowing that somehow I was blessed. I made it through with the help of a stripper pole. My family is safe. Even my house is still standing.

But these ladies, they're holding each other, crying, trying to reach their families on their phones. Nothing. We all stand and watch the black monster chewing up their town five miles away, and there's nothing else we can do until it moves on.

"Levi is in Deacon," Norm says.

Harley puts a hand on his shoulder. "We'll get there in a few minutes, Norm."

I look around and see Harley's and Norm's trucks. My Hummer is in a different part of the parking lot than where I parked it, but it's standing upright. Bruce's beer truck is gone. The van from the Second Baptist Church is under a tree, smashed in the middle like a pop can.

"It's almost over," Harley says as he points toward town. The storm has moved to the north, moving out over farmland and abandoned mines.

I dig in my bra, find my truck keys, and make my way to the Hummer. It fires up like a champ, and I pull it closer to the group and get out.

"I got Claude!" one of the women says, holding up her phone. "He's fine. Thank the Lord."

Two other women make similar exclamations as they reach their families by phone. Wilma Jack clears her throat. "Do any of them say if the police station is standing?"

The first woman is back on her phone, asking questions. "The post office and the library are gone, but the police station and the fire station are still there."

Wilma nods.

"So is the church," one of the other ladies says.

Beth Harper and another woman have their arms around each other, saying a prayer. They both try their phones again and, after a few attempts, put them back in their pockets. Beth looks at me. "Pratima can't reach her family. She talked to a neighbor and..." She doesn't finish. She doesn't have to.

"Have you reached Daze?"

She shakes her head. "I can't get Daze. Or Pet. Or Jerri Lynn." Her bottom lip is quivering. She's trying to stay strong. I may not agree with Beth Harper, but I understand that fear of not knowing if your family is okay, and my stomach hurts for her. I want to cry, but if she isn't going to, neither am I.

"Harley, take Sammie and Pratima and get to her house. See what you can do. Norm, drop these ladies at the church on your way in. It's going to be a busy place today."

Bruce jumps in the back of Norm's truck. "Drop me where I'm needed," he says.

On that, everyone starts moving, except Beth, who's still looking at me. "Come on, Beth. You're with me."

"There are so many people that will need help. I..."

"Yes, there are. And we could use Daze and Pet. So let's go find them first." She nods, a flicker of a smile, and lifts her chin as she walks to the Hummer.

Harley pulls his truck next to mine. I roll down my window.

"Tina, are you sure you're okay?"

"I'm alive. I'm fine. Now it's time to get to work."

FIVE MILES NORTH OF Deacon, in Springtown, the Spring River splits. The river runs behind the club and continues all the way to the Mississippi, I guess, but the tributary that cuts down from Springtown makes its way down farther west, forming the city limits of Deacon. By the time it gets to the road into Deacon, it's much more than just a creek, spanning a distance of at least thirty yards. To the locals, it's known as Beecher Creek, because the Beecher family has owned the land on one side of the bridge since the town was incorporated in the 1800s. They have a big house on the top of the hill next to the bridge, and on the hill lies a huge cross that they light at Christmas and Easter.

Harley is leading our convoy. Beth and I are in the back. As we make our way toward Deacon, I look up at the cross. It looks pale in the grayness of the day, lying on the hill.

Beecher's house is standing. It looks like the bridge is intact too. In times like this, it's important to notice the good as well as the bad. Just before we get to the bridge, Harley stops and turns around. He stops at Norm's truck and says a few words, and Norm turns around too.

"What's wrong?" Beth asks as she rolls down her window.

Harley pulls up beside us. "Water is pouring over the bridge. We need to go around, go in through Springtown," he says.

Beth looks at me. I look at the bridge. I can see the water, but it doesn't look like a lot to me. It's building, I know that, and I also know it doesn't take much to swipe a vehicle off the road and into the creek. But I don't turn around. I just sit there and look at the bridge. "It'll take another fifteen to twenty minutes if we go around." I don't really say this to Beth, more to myself. I look at Beth. And I look at the bridge.

"It doesn't look like much, Harley."

"It don't take much, Tina," he says.

"I know, but people need help." I look at Beth. She isn't saying anything, but I see a flicker of hope in her eyes, and I think about how I would feel if it were my family on the other side of that bridge. I'm usually a woman of reason, but sometimes, you have to have faith. There's no way I should be alive right now, but I am.

"You all go around. Beth and I are going over this bridge." Beth isn't saying a word, just looking at me while Harley starts to protest. I wave him off. "Harley, this Hummer weighs three tons. I have a full tank of gas, and with that and me and Beth, I figure we got close to another thousand pounds." I look across the bridge. Just then the Beechers turn the light on the cross, lighting up the Deacon side of the creek. I give Beth a big smile. "And we've got Jesus riding shotgun. We'll see you in Deacon." Beth holds out her hand, and I take it. She says a brief prayer then nods.

And I put the Hummer in drive and floor it.

HALFWAY ACROSS THE bridge, I begin to question my own decision. Water is spraying up to the windows on both sides of the truck.

I glance out my driver's side to see the swirling gray water of the creek rushing by, like a million rats crawling over one another, fighting for food. With twenty feet until the other side of the bridge, I feel the truck start to lift and realize I'm no longer in control. All I can do is hope that the forward momentum is enough to skim across the water without crashing into the side of the bridge or, worst case, into the water below. Beth says nothing, just keeps her eyes focused forward.

Then I feel the tires grip pavement, and I hit the brakes on the other side of the bridge, pulling the Hummer to a stop within inches of a large buffalo standing in the middle of the road. Beth and I say nothing. We look back at the bridge then at the buffalo then at each other. Seeing one of the herd from the Downstream standing in town a good five miles from its home may be strange, but we both know that will not be the strangest thing we'll see today. I call Harley. "We made it. Don't try it. We're on our way to Daze's house."

I drive slowly toward the center of town with Beth directing me to her house in between her praying. The streets are littered with broken cars, fallen trees, and the remains of several homes. I look to my right and see a mangled mess of what was once Deacon. To my left is a flattened plain with fewer houses standing than destroyed.

A few cars are weaving their way through the debris of the downtown area, and men and women are already searching through the mess. "Beth…" I don't know what to say, but the sound of my own voice is comforting in some way.

She's on her phone, trying to reach her family to no avail. I call Angus's number, and he answers on the first ring. Another silent prayer. "The fire department and police department are okay. They're organizing help parties right now," he says. I repeat that to Beth, who nods.

Finally, Beth directs me to the side of a residential street and has me pull over in front of a pile of lumber. A little dog is standing on top, barking at the ruin. There's a two-story historic home across the street, two empty lots, a ranch-style home that is split in the middle, more lots... I recognize Pet Harper's truck sideways in the road in front of a small house up ahead. "Which one is yours?"

She points at the pile of broken lumber with the little dog. I reach for her hand and force her to look into my eyes. She wipes her face, nods, and reaches for the passenger door handle.

Slowly, we walk across what was once a home. Beth calls to the dog, but he doesn't come. "That's Daze's dog. He loves that dog." She starts to cry again, and I put an arm around her.

"Where would they be?" I know, having lived in this area for most of my life, that most people have a plan for a storm: a shelter, a general area in the hallway, a bathroom. Beth points at the left side of the pile.

"The toolbox," she says. "Daze has a toolbox that's a makeshift shelter in the garage."

We pick our way slowly to where she assumes her garage used to be. The toolbox. I vaguely remember Daze mentioning that earlier. I take a deep breath and start throwing pieces of broken lumber away from the area, searching for a toolbox that's big enough to crawl into. Beth follows my lead. Two men and a woman come from nowhere and start digging with us, slowly, piece by piece, throwing lumber, only to find more wood and debris.

"Shhh." One of the men holds up a hand for us all to stop. We hear the steady thud, something banging against metal. It reminds me of my diamonds against the stripper pole less than an hour ago. "Over here," he says. The five of us dig in the area of the sound, and it gets louder with each layer of wood we remove. Then we reach shiny metal. "Got it!" And the sound is coming from inside.

"They're in there, Beth! Listen..." We clear the side where Beth tells us the trapdoor is, and it takes both men to pry the door open a few inches. They move more lumber, then the door bursts open from the inside. A teenage girl crawls from the mess, and Beth immediately embraces her. Behind her is Levi Dinger. I say another silent prayer.

Beth has tears of joy flowing freely, and I can't help but cry, too. We both look to the toolbox, waiting for Daze and Pet to crawl out next, but they don't come.

"They went back in, and they never came back," says Levi.

The girl, who Beth is calling Jerri, is screaming and pointing toward the pile of wood. She calls the little dog, who's still yapping. He doesn't come.

Levi climbs the pile of lumber and heads toward the dog, yelling for "Mr. Harper." The dog hasn't moved, and Levi starts slinging lumber like toothpicks from the spot where the little dog is barking. The rest of us join him and start moving the wood, relying on an old dachshund to show us the way.

"A bathtub," one of the men yells and points at the side of a white porcelain tub. Levi slings more wood from the top and pulls back a torn shower curtain. And there lie Daze and Pet, curled around each other like two twins in a womb.

"Thank you, Lord," Beth says as she claps her hands and turns her face to the sky.

"It's about time," Daze says as he crawls out of the tub. He hugs the teenage girl then puts a hand out to Pet. "And it looks like you owe me fifty dollars."

Pet looks at Jerri and Levi. "Well, I'll be. That toolbox sure did hold. Fifty bucks I'm happy to pay."

Standing on the pile of wood that was once their home, we look around the town of Deacon. Broken.

"Say, look there." Pet is pointing at the next street over. "My house is standing."

"At least we got a place to stay. But the rest of the town..." Daze pauses for a moment and shakes his head. He brushes his legs and arms. "Let's go. We got a lot of work to do. Jerri, you stick with Levi, and don't let her get in any trouble. Pet and I are gonna start right here in our neighborhood, then we'll move out to where we're needed."

He looks at me with a smile. "You think you could drop Beth at the church?"

"Sure," I say. "Then I'm going to find Benny and see where I can help. My Hummer should be useful."

I reach for Beth's hand and help her off the woodpile, and together, we head for my truck. Daze yells from behind us. "See, Beth, I told you Fat Tina was an okay gal."

Beth turns quickly with her hands on her hips. "Her name is Tina, Daze. Just Tina. And she's more than okay. She's an angel."

I have to smile as I step up in the Hummer. Me and Beth Harper.

The Lord certainly works in mysterious ways.

Chapter 16
Clay

When I was a kid, I used to lie in the backyard and look at the clouds. Big, fluffy white clouds that if you looked real hard, you could see a dog, or an airplane, or a dinosaur. I could lie there for hours, or what seemed like hours, just looking at the sky, smelling the grass, listening to the birds sing to one another in the trees. The clouds are dark today, one big cloud that changes from gray to black, and the only shape I can see is a vast nothingness, like looking in a deep hole in the ocean. The grass is wet, and I'm soaked to the bone. There aren't any birds singing.

It's not that I can't move. I haven't tried. I'm afraid to move. I'm afraid to look around, to see what the hell has happened. As long as I lie here and look at the clouds, there's nothing to fear. The minute I get up, I have to face reality. "Shaylene," I yell her name again. No answer. I can't look around. The nothingness is safe.

Babe Shatner told me to stay put, and I didn't listen. No, in the few minutes I had to make a decision about what would be safest for me and my daughter, I chose to listen to Maryanne and get in my truck and drive the few blocks to the nearest storm shelter. The responsible thing to do. But we didn't make it the three blocks. We barely made one before my truck was rolled over like a Tonka toy before slamming against the side of Lucky Dean's garage. But we were okay. Shook up, beat up, but okay. The three of us crawled out the driver's window, fighting the wind, trying to get inside Lucky's shop, but it was locked up, and we went for a ditch instead. I got on top of them both and wrapped my arms around Shaylene so tight I was afraid I would crush bone.

The storm was going over us. My back was being pummeled by wind, rain, and debris, but I kept my head down and held on to my daughter. It was all I could think about, my one job, one responsibility—hold on to Shaylene. Even when I felt us being lifted in the air, higher and higher, tumbling around like clothes in a dryer, I did not let go. *If we die, we'll die together*, I thought. *But she will not be alone. I will not let go.*

I woke up looking at the cloud above me. I don't know where I am, how I'm even alive, but I do know one thing: Shaylene is not in my arms. She's gone. And I'm afraid to look.

"Shaylene." I say her name again and listen. Nothing.

I shut my eyes and pray that sleep will come. I can't get up yet. I'm afraid.

She is gone.

And I am lost.

Chapter 17
Benny

It's over. It's just begun.

The station is standing, and I'm sitting on the concrete steps, listening to the sirens, watching people running in the street and wading through the rubble. Books are everywhere, most likely from the library across the street. One of Deacon's prizes, a three-story historic building that sits in the middle of an entire block, surrounded by a park for the patrons, gone now. So are most of the trees. I look up the flagpole that stands next to the steps. Old Glory is ripped like an old rag, but it's still waving.

And Jimmy is gone. I put my head between my knees and focus on a few stones that are on the concrete. He was there, smiling, holding a Chihuahua, and in a split second, he was a hundred feet up in the air and then just gone. I hear people yelling at me, but I don't look up. Screams come from every direction, covering me in little red dots like I'm the target for a town full of snipers. I lift my head and watch as if I'm in a tunnel. They keep yelling, and I keep turning away.

"Breaker, breaker. Anybody out there? We need all the help we can get here. So get your asses moving." Tenesy is in front of me, and he has my side radio. I watch. I don't care. Then he slaps me upside the head. "Snap out of it, dumbass." I can feel my eyes getting wet, but still, I don't move.

I don't care how old you are, when someone grabs your earlobe and starts twisting, you're going to get up and follow them wherever they lead. That's how Tenesy gets me in the building and in my office. Angus is there, and Tenesy flushes him out and shuts the door. The television is screaming and the front window is blown out, so I can still hear the chaos outside. He pushes me in my chair and leans over me so close I could punch him if I had the energy.

Tenesy sticks a finger in my face. "Listen here, Ruben. I don't know why all these people seem to think you're smart enough to run shit, but they do, and right now, they need someone who is going to take charge and get this mess handled. Sadly, that duty falls to you."

I look at him. He doesn't understand. "I need to call Grace," I say, fumbling for my phone.

"She's fine. I already talked to her. On her way from Joplin with a car full of nurses ready to dive in and help. There's a lot of folks out there. And some dead."

Jimmy. Jimmy's dead. I wipe my hand across my face.

Tenesy sits on the edge of my desk and gives me a little smirk. "You know why I'm such a good criminal? Because I always have a plan. Sure, sometimes, I gotta make it up as I go, but I don't just sit around and think, oh shit, what am I gonna do? 'Cause when you do that, you end up doin' nothin.'" He points out the open window. "You're in charge of this mess, and you ain't gonna fix it all, but you gotta start doin' something. If you sit on your ass and cry, that's what everyone else is going to do. You hear me?"

In his strange way, I know that Tenesy is trying to give me fatherly advice and be supportive. "Have you talked to Mom?" I ask.

He smirks again. "Yeah, I called her. Rudy answered the phone. She's fine, and he's got his guys guiding people into town from the west side."

"Rudy..."

Tenesy stops me. "Don't say nothin'. I'll deal with that shit later. In fact, the busier you can keep me today, the better chance Rudy has of livin' till morning."

The door to my office flies open, and standing there are Angus, R.T., and several others that had been taking cover in the jail, looking in at me, ready to dive in.

Tenesy stands up. "Let's go. I'll help ya."

"No." I stand up and open my desk drawer, take out a walkie, lay it on my desk, and take mine back from Tenesy. "You stay right here. I need solid hands out there and someone here that can take the calls and relay them to my guys." I come around my desk, and Tenesy takes my spot. I motion to the others standing there waiting to be told what to do. "Let's get to the firehouse. It's going to be easier if we're all working out of one station." The hallway starts to clear. I see my cowboy hat on the floor in the corner, grab it, and put it on. "Tenesy, by the way, you ain't a good criminal. Good criminals don't get caught."

"Go to work, dumbass," he says.

I walk out of the station and stand at the top of the stairs. I can hear the clink of the grommets beating against the flagpole, and I remind myself that our flag is still there. I look at the middle of the street, the last place I saw Jimmy. I shake it down; I'll deal with that later. Right now, I have a town to take care of. What's left of it, anyway.

Bucky Crow is already in motion. The regular men and the auxiliary firefighters are on post, and Bucky is relaying calls as they spread out all over town. He had one of his guys already at the community center, making sure it was secure to set up a makeshift clinic, and two others, both paramedics, in the garage of the fire station, already checking folks out. I tell Tenesy to keep relaying calls to me, and the ones that seem most urgent, I give to Bucky.

"Where do you need me, Bucky?" I like being the one in charge, don't get me wrong, but contrary to what my dad says, I'm not stupid. Bucky has the emergency equipment, and he's got this shit down.

Bucky stands about five foot five and probably about the same width. He reminds me of a concrete block, square and sturdy. He's full-blooded Choctaw and has one long, dark braid that hangs almost to his behind. He runs a clean department, makes sure his equipment is taken care of and his men stay well trained. Basically, he's one of the most solid guys I know, and right now, I'm thankful he's in Deacon.

He leads me into his office and shuts the door. We sit down and sketch out a plan, at least until the National Guard arrives. The mayor has already called for a state of emergency, but until then, we've got to do what we can.

"Let's get a list for Jimmy Ray of where to send people who are hurt or homeless, because a lot of those calls will be coming through you."

I swallow hard and shake my head. "Jimmy's gone." I can still see him and Schmegel, flying off, swept up like a piece of debris in the funnel. I push it back down.

"Damn. I'm sorry," Bucky says.

"Chief?" Angus is standing next to me with his phone in his hand. "Tina's in town helping at Daze Harper's. I can't get Maryanne or Shaylene."

Atta girl, Tina! "Go." I point toward the door. He doesn't hesitate and is gone before I can say anything else.

My radio blasts on my belt, and I answer it. Tenesy gets right to the point. "Lolly Beecher called and said there's some guy laying in the park, and the water's getting higher. She thinks he's still movin' but ain't gettin' up."

"On my way," I say.

Bucky points at my radio. "Is that your dad on the desk?"

"Yeah. Just got out this morning."

Bucky smiles. "No reason for him not to start a little community service right off the bat." He stands up and points at the garage. "Here they come. It's going to be a long week. You ready?" I look out at the garage, and five men are walking in, carrying rope and other supplies.

It's the four Sweeton boys with their daddy, Darrell. "Where do you need us?" the oldest asks.

Bucky smiles. "You men hunters?"

"Hell yes!" one of the boys says.

Bucky nods. "Ever try to catch a buffalo?"

I WEAVE MY WAY THROUGH what once was our town. Without my usual landmarks to guide me, I'm not even sure where I am half the time. Is this Twelfth Street? Where's the funeral home? And the houses? A few are there, but most are like piles of giant toothpicks. People are digging in the piles of wood, calling out names, looking, searching. A buffalo runs behind the nursing home. A buffalo. I shake my head.

"Jimmy, have someone check to make sure the nursing home residents are safe. The building looks fine, but someone needs to check on them, anyway. And tell Bucky the buffalo he's looking for is somewhere in that area." I put my walkie down on the seat next to me.

"10-4. And this ain't Jimmy, it's your daddy, dumb ass."

I pound my fists on my steering wheel until my hands start to go numb.

I damn near crash in to Maryanne Spencer as she runs in the middle of the road, waving her hands over her head, trying to flag me down. She's soaking wet and out of breath, and her clothes are ripped and dirty.

"Shaylene! She's gone. I can't find her! It picked us up and—" She's standing at my down window, and her eyes are darting back and forth like a crazy woman's.

"Slow down and get in. Angus is already looking for all three of you. I've got to grab some guy at the park, and then I'll take you back to Angus," I say.

"No, no! I've got to find her!" She opens the back door on the driver's side and gets in. "Take me to Angus, then go to the park. Please, Benny! She's my daughter."

I look at her in the rearview mirror and, for a second, want to break down and cry with her. I don't have any kids. Always wanted one but it just never happened, but I did have Jimmy, who was about as close as I guess I'm going to get. I shake off the feeling of giving in; I've got to stay strong. There are a lot of people who need help right now. "Angus is on it. I'll let him know I've got you. The park is just a few blocks up. We'll grab the guy there and get you both back to the community center."

"But—"

I've already got the Tahoe in drive and try to shut out her protests. As I turn just before the bridge over the river to go down into the park, I look up on the hill at the giant cross that has been there since I can remember. It's lit up like Easter, and I take a little comfort in that.

Chapter 18
Clay

When Shaylene was five, I took her to Joplin to the carnival that was set up outside of town. It was just Shaylene and me, one of the rare occasions when I had her all to myself for an entire day. We played games until I finally won her a giant panda that was bigger than she was. We ate junk food until we were ready to puke. We rode every ride she was old enough to get on.

Her favorite was the carousel. She ran through the maze of unicorns, fire-breathing dragons, and giant fireflies until she found the one that was just right for her, a pink horse with wings that went up and down as the ride turned. I helped her on then stood beside the carousel and waved at her each time she came around. With her long brown hair blowing in the wind and a smile the size of Texas, Shaylene was waving to me like she was washing a giant window—up and down, up and down on her magical flying horse.

On about her fifth ride, I was standing in my usual spot next to a green bench, waiting for her to come around. I saw the nose of the pink Pegasus, but as it circled, Shaylene wasn't there. I waited for it to make another complete circle, thinking she had somehow changed horses while the ride was in motion, but she wasn't there. She was gone. I jumped on the moving ride, to the disapproval of the carny in charge, and ran among the other children, yelling her name. Gone.

You always hear on the news how some psycho takes a kid from someplace like that, and usually, you shake your head and wonder what kind of parent wouldn't keep their eye on their own kid. But I did. I was right there. I ran frantically around the carousel. The carny finally stopped the ride, and we looked for her. I remember thinking about how I was going to tell Maryanne that I had lost our child, how Roland would be an ass about it and laugh. The pit of my stomach was full, and I wanted to puke, to cry, to punch something, but most of all, I just wanted my little girl back.

"Daddy." And there she was. Standing on the other side of the carousel, next to a bench just like the one on the other side. She had been going around, saw the bench, and thought it was the one that I was at but didn't see me there. She crawled off her magical horse and got off, jumped off, to try to find me. Five years old and she was looking for me. "I thought I lost you."

Now, I lie on my back, somewhere by the river, not wanting to open my eyes, trying to stay in that memory of finding her. I hurt all over, but the numbness in my heart trumps everything else. My biggest responsibility was to keep her safe, and I almost blew it that day.

"Where is she?" I turn my head to see Maryanne jumping out of Benny's cruiser. Benny is right behind her, and when they get to me, Maryanne drops to the ground next to me and starts shaking my shoulder. "Where is she?" she screams.

"I had her," I say, then I slowly shake my head. *All I had to do was hold on. But I had her. I had her...*

Maryanne gets up and begins screaming Shaylene's name and running through the park. I know I should be looking too, but I also know that once I leave this place on the ground, it all becomes real. I'm still hoping this is nothing but a bad dream.

I feel a hand on my shoulder and open my eyes again to see Benny Cloud looking down at me. His face is bright red, and he's sweating like he's just run a race.

"Clay, can you move?"

I can, but I don't want to. I nod.

"Let's sit up," Benny says.

He grabs me under the arm and helps me to a sitting position, and I clutch my right thigh when pain radiates through my leg and hip and feels like I've been shot with a flaming arrow. I fall down on my back and try not to scream. My head is turning like a carousel, and it hurts like hell.

"Just lie here another minute," Benny says. I'm fine to do just that.

"Tenesy, I need you to get hold of Angus and tell him I got Clay Adams too. And get me an ambulance down here. He's busted up pretty bad."

My leg is vibrating, and I try to ignore it. I turn my head and see that Benny is talking on his walkie. He puts a hand on my arm and squeezes. "But no sign of the girl." *The girl. Shaylene. We were caught up in a tornado, round and round. Then she was gone.* I can hear Maryanne, in the distance, calling her name.

"Everyone in town seems to need an ambulance. I got a woman standin' here named Tina that says to tell you she's on her way. I guess that's the only ambulance you're gonna get for a while."

Benny lowers his head and lets out a slow breath. "That'll have to do," he says in the walkie. I lie there, listening to the sound of the river rushing by and Maryanne yelling in the distance. Benny sits next to me, waiting.

I start digging in my pockets for my phone. "Cassie..." Cassie and Babe were at the house, and...

Benny pulls his phone out and hands it to me. I take several deep breaths and dial Cassie's number. She answers on the first ring, and I hit the button to put her on speaker.

"Are you okay?" I ask.

"Why are you calling me on Benny Cloud's phone?" Of course that's the first thing Cassie would say.

"I've got a broken leg." I can't tell her everything. Not yet. I can't even describe it to myself. I can't—

"You've also got another mouth to feed," she says.

"What?" Then I realize what she's trying to tell me. I try to sit up again but fall back when the pain forces me down. Benny has a sad smile on his face and slaps me gently on the arm.

"I've been trying to get you, but your phone isn't working. Grams said you'd be fine if you just stayed at Maryanne's house, so I wasn't too worried."

I flinch when she says that and pat my leg. The vibration. My phone. Damn. "You had the baby at home? Is he okay? Cassie, I—"

"*She* is just fine. Perfect. I named her already. Stormy Em. Is that okay?"

I nod. *A girl. I have another girl.* "I love it. It's a good name, a strong name."

"Grams is packing us up to drive us to the hospital in Columbia. Are you on your way home?"

I look at Benny, who shakes his head. "Tell her to go to Joplin. Columbia is going to be overloaded."

"Cassie, I don't want you to get riled up when I tell you this, but I kind of got hurt and—" *Shaylene.*

"How hurt?" she asks.

"I broke my leg. And my hip doesn't feel too good either. Benny's sending me to the hospital in Joplin. But that's not the worst of it." I swallow hard and blink several times.

"Where's Maryanne?" she asks.

"Maryanne?" I had forgotten about Cassie's dream and my promise to look out for her.

Benny stands and points upriver. "I'll go get her."

"Maryanne's fine. But Shaylene..." I can't say the words.

Cassie is not one to be at a loss for words. But there's dead silence on the line. I know she loves Shaylene, and the thought of losing one daughter on the same day you get another is more than I think either of us can bear. "Cassie," I whisper, "I had her. And she's not here. Angus is looking for her, but..."

A baby cries in the background, and I want to laugh and cry at the same time. A car door slams, and I look over to see Tina Early coming toward me.

"You still there, Cassie?"

The phone beeps in my hand, and out of habit, I look down to see who's calling. It's Angus, then I remember I'm on Benny's phone. "Angus is calling. I gotta go. I love you, and I'll see you at the hospital." I hit the answer button on Benny's phone just as Tina squats down next to me.

"Angus, it's Clay," I say.

"I got her. She ran into town to get help for you and went to the community center!"

"You? What? Shaylene?" I'm not sure I heard him correctly or if my mind is playing tricks on me.

Then I hear her voice. "Daddy? Are you okay?"

I start laughing. "I am now."

"You scared me! You wouldn't wake up, and I had to pry myself away from you to run into town for help. Don't do that!"

Pried herself away from me. I smile. I held on.

"Angus said Mom's okay? She's with you?" She sounds so excited. Full of life.

"She's fine. And Cassie is fine. And you have a new sister," I say. "Call her when we hang up and tell her you are fine, please."

She squeals, and despite the pain in my lower body, I want to squeal with her.

"Tenesy said Tina was on her way to the park." Angus is back on the phone. He doesn't sound nearly as excited as I feel right now, and despite my own happiness that my family is intact, I sense that the town is in bad shape.

"She's right here. Thanks, Angus, for everything." I hand the phone to Tina.

"I'm going to run Clay over to Joplin after Benny and I get him in my truck. Then Maryanne can ride back to town with him." She pauses and looks at me. "Where's Benny?"

I point upriver in the direction he headed to get Maryanne. Tina turns to look that way then drops the phone and takes off running across the park.

How quickly things can go from bad to good to worse.

Chapter 19
Benny

There are a few things in life that you always know in the back of your mind could happen, but you really don't expect them to. Becoming a diabetic at forty. Cass Adams having a baby. An F-5 tornado flattening your town. But here we are, and damned if I wasn't prepared for any of it. Not that Cass is my responsibility, but maybe I'm a little jealous. I'm happy for Clay and glad the baby is doing okay, but it just seems so typically Cass for her to have one of the best days of her life on the day that Deacon is facing so much death and heartache.

Or maybe I'm just trying to find a way to forget about Jimmy for a little while. I look back at Clay lying on the wet grass. He was lifted up and thrown damn near a mile, so maybe Jimmy is lying in a park somewhere, watching Schmegel wheeze. I'll hold on to that image—at least until this is all over.

But not everyone is going to be as lucky as that. Maryanne Spencer is about fifty yards upriver, looking in the water for her daughter, screaming her name over and over. She's not going to like me reining her back, but she's getting too close to the water, and the last thing I need today is to have to fish one out.

I stop for a second and wipe my brow and catch my breath. I probably should have brought one of those cardboard protein bars that Grace gave me, because I'm not feeling too good. I've had heartburn all day, and now I feel worn slick.

Tenesy's voice comes across my walkie. "Some guy named Harvey just called in and said he's helpin' Bucky Crow's boys out at the mop factory." I nod but don't respond. I hadn't heard from Harvey since before this thing hit, and it's a relief to know he made it through.

I reach for my phone to give Grace a call and remember I left it with Clay. Damn, I promised her I'd be home tonight at seven for her big surprise, and even though I know she won't expect it now, I still need to tell her I'm sorry to have to miss it. It's one of those little things you do when you have a good wife: tell her you're sorry when it isn't really necessary. Or maybe I just need to hear her voice right now.

I continue walking across the park, keeping an eye on Maryanne. Instead of walking up the bank of the river, she's stopped and is standing on a fallen tree that extends out into the water. I can't see what she's looking at, but I know if she gets too far out, she could fall in. Or the damn trunk could shift, and she'd be up a creek without a paddle—literally. "Maryanne!" I yell as loud as I can to get her attention, but she doesn't seem to hear me, or maybe she doesn't care.

"Shit," I say and double my pace to get to her.

My jaw aches, like I've just been gnawing on a shoe-leather steak. I move my jaw around, listening to it pop. I'm sweating, even though it can't be more than seventy degrees outside. I stop walking again and look up and see the gray clouds swirling like a pinwheel and feel a few sprinkles of rain on my cheeks. I unzip my jacket and wait for the next breeze to come through, then I bend forward a little to catch my breath again. *Damn, how can I be this out of shape?*

I stand up, looking toward Maryanne, and just as I get to full height, a sharp pain like I've been hit with a sledge hammer slams me in the chest and shoots up to my shoulder and down my left arm. I grab my chest. It's hard to breathe. I close my eyes, and when I open them, I'm looking across the river at a grove of trees. I'm dizzy and my legs buckle, and I can't help but fall to the ground on bended knee.

I call for help, but it comes out as only a whisper. My chest is tightening even more, and I fall on the ground, landing on my right side, facing the river. Maryanne Spencer is halfway out that tree trunk, and I'm not going to get to her. I hear Tenesy on the walkie on my side, calling me, but I can't make my arm move toward it. I swear I can hear Grace somewhere in the distance, calling my name. But I'm alone and I'm dying, and there isn't anything I can do about it.

I lie there, trying to breathe, trying to keep my eyes open. A shadow covers me. "Grace?" I don't know if I actually say it or just think it. I look up and see Roland Adams, and all I can think is *Damn, he don't look too bad for a dead guy.*

Then I'm on my back, looking up into Tina's face. She's shaking me, and her mouth is moving, but I can't hear her. I point toward the river. "Get her." She looks off then back at me, and I nod one time.

I blink, and Tina is gone. There's someone else, or some*thing*, next to me, rubbing my chest. I can't look at her face, but I know it's a woman because she's gentle, and I feel better because she's there. I shut my eyes for what seems like just a minute. Then everything is still. I'm still. I can't feel anything. I open my eyes, and I'm staring at the giant cross that is lit up on the side of Beecher Hill.

I'm so sorry, Grace.

I shut my eyes and let God do what she wants.

Chapter 20
Maryanne

I grew up in Kansas, so it's not like this was my first tornado. My house has withstood many years of the weather, and I know that most of the time, I'm just as safe there as I am in a shelter. The last time I went to Archie's shelter, it was packed with other Deacon residents crying and wailing worse than the sixth graders I teach, and many of whom I'd swear hadn't bathed in a week. But today, Shaylene was with me, and I didn't want to take any chances.

Damn! I know better than to be out in it when it's so close! I saw it drop out of the sky before the sirens went off. I know the winds can do enough damage, and the actual funnel, well, it can lift you up and rip you to pieces or throw you halfway across town. And that's exactly what happened.

I move through the park at a fast pace. Looking. Looking. Calling her name. I look in the shrubbery, in the trees, on every structure in the park and in every nook and crevice I can find. Nothing. I look to the swollen river running swiftly downstream and risen so high it's one good rain from jumping its bed. *If she landed in the water...*

I know Clay is hurt and probably pretty bad since he's just lying there, but at this point I have one concern: finding my daughter. I was in the ditch, she was on top of me, and Clay on top of her, holding on. *Why was I on the bottom? How the hell did Clay not hold on to her?* I want to go back to him and kick him for letting her go, but if he landed here, she may have landed close by. *Please, God, don't let her be dead. She's all I have.*

I stumble on a large boulder that I didn't see because I was watching the water. I pick myself back up and start moving upstream. Things are bobbing on the water: a large tree limb, a smashed-up jon boat that someone didn't have tied down very well, a washing machine. But no Shaylene. And no body.

I wipe the tears from my face and, with them, wipe away the idea that she could be dead. No. I've already lost. I lost Roland last year, and it's not fair if something happens to Shaylene. I look to the heavens and scream, "It's not fair!" but keep moving and scanning the water.

Angus is looking for her, Benny had told me, which means he's okay. Of course he's looking. That would be Angus's first thought: of me and Shaylene. How odd that I'm just now thinking of him. I push that thought away and keep moving. Angus can wait.

I look back at where I left Benny and Clay, and Benny is walking my way. He's still more than half a football field away. He yells my name, but I ignore him and turn toward the river.

Then I see it.

A large tree trunk has fallen and extends out into the water about ten feet. At the end, tangled in its gnarly branches, is a bright-blue fabric. A shirt? Shaylene was wearing a bright-blue Jayhawks T-shirt. I try to get as close as I can, but I can't tell. I need to know. The trunk is easily five feet in diameter, and it's not moving. I climb on and start crawling toward the end. I need to get close enough to see it.

When I'm six feet over the water, I realize I may have made a grave mistake. Water is slapping against the bottom of the trunk and flowing around it. It wouldn't take much for it to start flowing over it, and if I fall in, there's nothing to stop me from washing up on the shore somewhere between here and the Twin Bridges in Oklahoma. I glance toward Clay, who is still on the ground, and don't see Benny any more. Tina Early is moving in my direction. *Where the hell did she come from?*

With one more hard look at the fabric that was my destination, I see a yellow sunflower and realize it's a Kansas state flag, blown from its pole somewhere upstream, fighting to hold its ground and stay away from the Oklahoma line. Defeat and relief flow through me at the same time, and as I slowly start to inch my way backward on the trunk, I'm afraid.

I glance back. I'm only a foot away from the shore; I can make it. As I turn, the trunk shifts and rolls enough to the right that no matter how hard I try to stay on top, I'm thrown off the log and into the water.

I'm close to the shore. I should be able to touch bottom here, but I can't. The water is too high, and it's moving too fast, and I can't place my feet. I'm reaching for the shore, anything to hold on to, but I can't grab anything. I'm treading, trying to stay above the water, taking too much of it into my mouth when I submerge and spitting it out as I resurface. But I'm moving, and fighting, and trying to hold my breath, then the feeling of hot lava fills my throat. And darkness.

I'm lying on a beach, the waves rushing over me, reaching higher and higher. There's a pain in my chest, and as I rub it, it goes numb. I can't move, and I'm alone, but I'm not afraid. I look out over the water. The sun is getting brighter and brighter, and the warmth of it caresses my body. A figure is coming toward me, out of the water, only a silhouette against the sun, but I feel no threat, only peace. I know who it is before I even see his face. I wait.

Up until a year ago, my entire adult life has been spent waiting for one man to take me away, to leave everything behind and take me off into the sunset. To paradise. To our own heaven. To just grab me by the hand and say, "Let's go." And I waited, knowing, when that time finally came, I'd be ready, no questions, no need to pack a bag. I look up and see the big blue eyes, the curly brown hair, the dimple digging deep into his chin under a smile bright as the sun.

Roland puts his hand out for me. "Let's go."

Our fingertips touch, then I'm doubled over like I've been hit in the stomach by an invisible blow. I hear my name and look behind me. A rainbow with colors I never before imagined. I turn back to Roland and shake my head.

I'm not ready.

I'm coughing and trying to catch my breath, and fighting again, fighting to stay above the water, but I realize I'm not in the water anymore. I'm on the ground. Tina Early is over me, her hands in the middle of my chest—*holding me down?* My throat burns. I cough and spit out water that tastes like dirt and cough some more. I try to sit up, but Tina rolls me over on my side and tells me to stay there. I do.

The blue water of the ocean is now the dark-gray Spring River. There is no rainbow, just grayness. And there is no Roland. My stomach hurts, my chest hurts, my throat hurts, my head hurts.

But I'm alive. I know I'm alive.

Tina is talking to someone. "I need an ambulance out here right now. I got three people that need to go, and I can't do it by myself."

Three? Shaylene? I roll over to see who she's talking to, and she's standing with a walkie-talkie in her hand. I also see Benny Cloud lying on the ground twenty feet away from me.

"Can't do it, lady. Unless it's life or death, they gotta wait," the voice on the other end of the walkie-talkie replies.

"Tina," I barely manage to get out, and it hurts to talk, and I slowly sit up.

"Stay there," Tina commands loudly. I stay and try to focus on Benny.

"Tenesy, I'm calling you on my phone, and I need you to pick it up. You understand?" she says.

"I ain't got time for—"

"Just do it!" She throws the walkie on the ground. She reaches down the top of her dress and pulls her cell phone out of her bra and punches it a few times. She's keeping her voice low, and I strain to hear bits and pieces.

"Tenesy... Heart... Tell Grace... I'm sorry..."

When she gets off the phone, I look up, and she's covered her face with her hands, and tears are flowing through her fingers. I look again at Benny, lying on his back.

"Tina," I ask, "is he...?"

"Dead," she says. "Benny is dead."

Chapter 21
Cass

It's almost nine o'clock, and my hospital room has finally cleared out of visitors—all except Maryanne. I'm not really tired, but it has been a long day. By the time Clay got to the hospital, Stormy was in the nursery, and I had had my privates checked and was moving to a room. I got to see him briefly as they wheeled him to surgery, and I waited it out standing at the window in front of the nursery, watching the nurses make my baby cry. I was tired but also full of energy, if that can happen, and I needed to know that Clay was okay before I rested.

His surgery went well. He's a bit of a mess, but he'll heal, and he still hasn't gotten to see his daughter. His room is on a different floor than mine, and I figure I'll sneak up there once my room is no longer a swinging door for those with issues.

Clay had called me after they got him and Maryanne loaded in an ambulance. Shaylene had been at the fire station when the call came over and was smart enough to hitch a ride with the paramedics before they headed for the river. Clay told me about Maryanne, and Benny, and how hard the town was hit, but my biggest concern was, and still is, him. A broken leg and a broken hip, but he'll recover. Maryanne drowned—like I didn't see that coming—but then she came back like a bad rash. But Benny Cloud—well, that's another story.

I never liked Benny much. In fact, ever since I beat him up in grade school, we haven't been what you'd call friends. And of course, last year when he threw me in jail, I liked him a whole lot less. But that don't mean I wanted to see him dead. Grams is really broken up about it, and I figure Clay and Maryanne will be, too, so I'm trying my best to keep the fact that I'm full of joy to myself. This could easily be the greatest day of my life.

"Angus said the town is really a disaster," says Maryanne. She hasn't left the hospital since she got here. They wanted to keep her overnight, but when she said no, they didn't fuss. They need all the empty beds they can get right now.

"Where is he? Why hasn't he come to get you yet?" I ask.

She shrugs and looks away. "Bobby Leo is coming to pick me up so Angus can work. Without Benny and Jimmy..."

I look at her sideways. I think there's more to it than that. Her house is just fine. In fact, if they had listened to Grams, none of them would be in the mess they're in, and she could have ridden back to town with Lola and Grams an hour ago like Shaylene did. But she stayed here.

"And?" I don't really care. But I know that when Maryanne wants to talk about herself, which is always, it's best to let her say what she wants and get it over with. I want it over with. I'm ready to go up and see Clay then say good night to Stormy and get some sleep.

"I saw Roland," she says. Her voice is raspy, and she acts like she's really weighing what she wants to say.

My stomach does a somersault when she says this. I want to ask her if he was on a beach, and I want to know if it was just like my vision, but I also don't want her to know I saw it coming and said nothing.

Instead, I start laughing. "He's still dead, isn't he?"

"He was there. When I drowned. He wanted me to go with him, but I didn't. I..."

I shake my head. Here's a woman who had a kid with my husband nineteen years ago and didn't tell a soul, then she pined after him up until the day I killed him. And now she's sitting here telling me he came for her when she died, and she turned him down. Well, at least maybe she's wisened up in a year and realizes that even in death, he's an asshole.

"It's just that..." She pauses as if thinking about her words. "I still love him, but I've got something to live for."

"How do you still love him? He's dead. You damn sure do have something to live for. Shaylene. And Angus. A good man, plus he's actually alive." I swear, if she hurts Angus, I may have to kill her myself.

She shakes her head. "No. It's me. I have me to live for. I waited around for Roland, for a man, to make me happy. And now, I'm expecting another man to do it? No."

Of course. It's all about her. I should have known how this was going to end. "You're going to break his heart."

She shrugs again. I hate that shrug. "Better his than mine, I guess. He'll be fine. He needs to find a good woman who can give him what he wants. Be faithful. But it's not me."

I fall back on my pillow and let out a long breath. "So, what are you going to do?"

She clears her throat and shrugs. Again. "Live."

"SO I HAD YOU WATCH over her to keep her from dying, and now all she wants to do is 'live.' How's that for typical Maryanne?" I'm sitting next to Clay's bed, holding his hand, trying to do all the talking so he doesn't have to. He's tired, and I know he's hurting, but he manages to give me a weak smile. I know I should give him time to rest, but I haven't been alone with him since he left for work this morning, and a lot has happened since then.

I also needed to vent to someone about Maryanne, and without Grams handy, and with Clay a captive audience, he wins. Or loses. I didn't want her to die, and she didn't, so I should be happy about that, but there's something else that pisses me off about it, and I can't quite put my finger on it.

"Lola?" His voice is soft, and he has to take a drink after saying my sister's name.

"She got here while you were in surgery. She says Stormy looks like her, which is fine by me, but I really think she's going to look like you." Honestly, she's only a few hours old, and I don't see it. She's pale with a smidgen of blond hair, and her eyes are gray. She doesn't look like anyone but Stormy to me.

"Benny Cloud—"

I shake my head. There are several people who've been hurt today and a few, including Benny, who didn't make it. For the next several months, the entire town is going to be turned upside-down, and I know Clay will want to be right in the middle of helping out—at least as much as he can while he's trying to recover. But tonight, I don't want to talk about Deacon, or Benny, or whose house is standing or not. Our family is alive and, for the most part, doing okay. And we have a beautiful baby girl that Clay hasn't met yet.

He takes my hand and squeezes it, and I get up and kiss him on the forehead. "They're kicking me out of here tomorrow. I'll bring Stormy to meet you in the morning, and I'll be here every day until they send you home too. We'll have to stay with Grams for a little bit until the windows are replaced, but we'll probably need the extra help anyway for a few weeks." *Or months,* I think. Clay's doctor said that his surgery went well, but he'll have a long way to go until he's back to normal. Clay laid up, a newborn, Dog, and me trying to adjust to all the newness. Yeah, Grams is going to be busy.

I turn to walk to my room, but Clay pulls me back. "I love you," he whispers.

I nod. "Me too. And thanks for not dyin.'"

Chapter 22

Tina

What the hell happened? I've gone over it in my mind, time and time again, and I still can't quite wrap my head around it. I keep replaying the events of yesterday afternoon, trying to make excuses or shift the blame, but no matter how I spin it, I let Benny die. My friend. I left him lying in the grass, obviously having a heart attack, to save a woman who doesn't give a spit for me.

Could I have saved him? Maybe, maybe not. But walking away, leaving him there on the grass so I could pull Maryanne out of the water, there was no chance of me helping him. She was dead, too, by all accounts, and she had done it to herself. Why? Because he told me to? I shake my head and pull out my old coffeemaker from under the counter. I've been Keurig-ing all night, and the way I'm going through it, I'm better off to make it by the pot.

I wait for my coffee, pour myself a mug, and walk out on the patio to a golden sun shining through a bright-blue sky. Sonja is already there, pouring cereal in bowls for Eb and Augie. She stayed last night, and after I kissed them to the point of embarrassing them, I stayed in my room, venturing out for something to drink every now and then, watching the news from Deacon on the TV, crying not only for the loss of my friend but also for all the people in town. *I need to be there helping,* I told myself at least a dozen times, but couldn't bring myself to actually get up and go. I'd done enough.

"Where's Dad?" Augie asks between bites. He's got Harley's gray eyes and thin nose but has a build like me, even at ten.

"He's sleeping. He got home a few hours ago." Harley has been out all night, calling me to check in every few hours, making sure I was okay. I lied each time. *I'm fine.*

After tipping the bowl and drinking all the milk, Eb jumps up, kisses me on the cheek, then looks at Augie. "Let's go!"

"Whoa. Go where? I thought you were sick?" I stop him.

"That was yesterday, Mom. I'm fine now," he says.

Augie finishes his breakfast and stands too. "Grandma is coming to pick us up. The school's closed for the week, and she said you and Dad probably need a few days to do some things."

I give Sonja a look that says, *When did this happen?*

"She talked to Harlan last night. With the schools closed and the club—"

The schools are closed? How did I miss that? Then I think: *Of course they're closed. Downtown Deacon looks like a bomb exploded in it.* I nod and try to smile for the boys. They love going to Grandma Early's house. She treats them like little princes, and I swear, the woman doesn't know how to say no.

"Sorry about the club," Augie says.

The boys know what I do. They know what the club is about. Harley and I have made a point of being very open with them about it, not trying to rose-color the world, even if they are young. We both believe that doesn't do them any good later in life. But how they really feel about my business, I've never asked.

I wave my hand in the air dismissively. "It's just a building." *But Benny, he was more than a building.*

Sonja follows the boys. I wonder where Sammie is. Sleeping? Helping in town? *I need sleep. I need more coffee. I need to wake up and this all be a bad dream.*

"Hey, Sis, I've been worried about you." I'm shaken from my thoughts by Angus's voice. I didn't even hear him come in. He's got a twenty-four-hour growth of beard, his hair is nappy, and his uniform is torn and filthy. He looks ten years older and not like the crisp, clean Angus who usually walks in my door. "I was hoping you were sleeping, but looking at you, it doesn't look like you've done much of that."

"I could say the same."

He tries a smile. "Well, I've been a little busy. And I don't have an apartment anymore, so I was hoping I could borrow a shower and crash on your couch for a few hours."

Oh no. I've been so wrapped up in my own grief, I didn't even think about Angus's shop. "I'm sorry. I didn't know."

"I guess we'll just have to start over together," he says as he sits at the patio table with me.

"Is Maryanne's house gone too?" I don't mind Angus staying here but wonder why he would want to, unless Maryanne's house has been destroyed as well.

"No, no. I haven't talked to her, and don't want to assume—"

"You haven't talked to her at all?" Something isn't right. This doesn't sound like the Angus I know.

"I talked to her for a few minutes while she was at the hospital yesterday. They were checking her out, and she wanted to stay with Cass and Clay, and like I said, I've been busy. Don't make more of it than it is." But instead of looking at me when he says this, he's looking out over the water, and I sense it is more than it is.

I'm so mad I'm afraid to say anything. What he sees in her, I'll never know. She's a self-centered bitch if you ask me.

Angus pats my arm, getting my attention again. "I know it's hard with Benny gone, and I'm not really sure what all happened down there yesterday, but thank you for saving Maryanne. You're my hero, you know."

I shake my head. *No. No.* "I didn't save anybody," I say. "Benny pulled her out of the water and pumped her chest and then had a heart attack. All I did was call Tenesy on the walkie." It all just spills out, and the more I say, the more I want it to be true.

He cocks his head and squints at me. "Maryanne said—"

"She's lying," I snap back. "She was dead herself. I'm not sure her recollection is considered reliable."

He holds his hands up defensively. "Sorry, I... Can I use the couch?"

I nod. "Of course. I'm sorry, I'm a little shaken from everything. The boys are going to Harley's mom's for a few days, so take Augie's room. Stay as long as you like."

He kisses me on the forehead and says, "Thanks, Sis. We'll get through this. I promise."

After he leaves, I shut my eyes and try to tame the anger rising in me. Maryanne Spencer. I get to tell this story, and if she even thinks of saying different, especially to Grace—

"So that's the story you're going with." I turn, and Harley is standing in the doorway with a cup of coffee in his hand.

"I thought you were sleeping?" I say.

"I was, but I got a lot to do. Don't change the subject. That's your story?"

"It's the truth. Benny saved her, not me."

He nods and sits down at the table with me. "How are you this morning?"

I feel horrible. I'm hurt, angry, confused. I watched my friend die, my business is gone, and I didn't even know my kids were leaving with their grandmother. I'm useless, pitiful. Broken. "I don't know," I say.

He reaches out and holds my hand. "You know, it wouldn't hurt if you talked to someone. Help you sort it out."

"You mean like a therapist?" *Great, and now my husband thinks I'm weak.*

"It's not a bad thing," he says.

"I need to call Grace." My chest hurts when I say her name.

"Yeah," he says. "Tell her what happened. It'll make sense to her that Benny died trying to save someone else. He died a hero."

I don't really want to talk to anyone, especially not to Benny's wife, but I know it's the right thing to do, and I would rather get it over with. *I don't mean it like that. It will never be over with.* I ask Harley if I can use his phone and dial Benny's home number. His name pops up on the screen, and I almost hit End instead of Send.

"Hello?" She sounds distant, an echo in a cave. *Or maybe she's just hollow on the inside, like me.*

"Grace? It's me, Tina." I stop for a minute and swallow hard. "I'm so sorry." And then I'm crying. Again. Harley hands me a napkin, and I wipe my face and try to continue.

"I don't know what to say, Grace. I don't know what happened, it just..." That's not true. I do know what happened. "If you need anything, Harley and I are just a call away."

"Benny's parents are here." Her tone is flat, and she doesn't sound like Grace at all.

"I need to tell you what happened," I say.

"Who's talkin'?" It's another voice, a man's voice, one I recognize. Tenesy Cloud, Benny's dad.

"It's Tina Early, Mr. Cloud." *Grace doesn't want to talk to me?* I think about hanging up, but he speaks before I can.

"Yesterday it was Tenesy, and I reckon that's where it should stay. Gracie took a sleepin' pill and damn near dropped the phone. Josie is putting her to bed right now. I'm supposed to just tell everyone thanks for callin', but since it's you..."

When I told Tenesy what happened on the phone yesterday, he only hesitated for a second. He sent an ambulance for Clay and Maryanne and somehow found a guy from Springtown with a van to pick up Benny and take him to the funeral home in Columbia. Then, according to Harlan, he turned the walkie-talkie over to Bucky Crow and went to tell Grace and Benny's mother. After everyone was gone, I was left in the park and sat in my Hummer and cried until I was dry. Then I drove home and have been here ever since.

"Thank you for what you did yesterday. I know it had to be hard to hear."

"Helluva 'welcome home from prison' party," he says. *Helluva response*, I think. Benny told me he was... different, and now I kind of know what he meant.

"Tenesy, I need you to tell Grace what happened. It all was so fast. Benny pulled Maryanne out of the water and resuscitated her. Then he grabbed his chest and fell to the ground. I tried to help him, but—"

"*He* pulled her out?" he asks. "You sure about that?"

Of course I'm sure. Sure that's the way I want it to be. "Yes, he saved her before he—"

"Huh. I'll be sure and tell Gracie and Josie. They'll like hearing that."

He doesn't sound like he believes me, but I don't care. As long as he tells the story *my* way.

"Dyin' a hero. Yeah, that will make it some better."

"Yes. Benny is a hero," I say with finality.

That's the story I want told.

Chapter 23
Maryanne

Roland had told me many times there were good reasons for him not having a child with Cass. He already had Shaylene, even if he didn't claim her. He didn't want to be tied to Cass forever, even though he never left her. And the biggest one of all: she was mentally unstable, and he was afraid she'd do something to harm the kid, or worse, in his opinion, she'd do something like her mother did, and he'd be left raising it. I believed him. I believed anything Roland told me. But now, watching Cass with Stormy, I realize how wrong he was. Cass is going to be a good mom, and in just the two days since Stormy has been here, I see a change in her. She's calm, she's happy, and she's head over heels in love with that baby.

Lola had to about pry Stormy from her hands to put her down for a nap. Then Lola decided she needed to hold her and rock her before she actually put her in the crib. And Babe Shatner is in another world, with Lola, Cass, and Stormy staying in her house right now. These women needed a baby.

"They moved Clay to that new rehab place in Springtown this morning. After Stormy gets her nap, we're going to go visit her daddy," Cass says.

"That was fast! I figured they'd keep him at least for a week."

She shrugs. "They need the beds. And besides, the sooner he gets started in rehab, the sooner he can get home. Well, here, Grams's house. Ours won't be ready for a while."

Clay's house didn't sustain a lot of damage, but the windows were almost all blown out. That's what he gets for using cheap windows. The carpet will need to be replaced, too, and with Clay laid up for a few months and everyone in town needing work done, it may be a while.

"Have you seen Angus?" I ask. I know the shop is gone, and it's not like Cass would be going to work, anyway, after just having a baby, but she and Angus are friends.

"Of course. He stopped by to check on us and meet Stormy. He looks shot, but wait. Don't tell me you haven't seen him?"

I don't say anything and now wish I hadn't asked.

"I talked to him at the hospital. We've been busy," I say.

"That was two days ago!" She rolls her eyes and shakes her head as if I'm a child and she's the disappointed mommy. "He may have been busy, but you've been doing what?"

"Taking care of Shaylene. I have responsibilities, too, you know."

"Shaylene is a grown woman. Your house is fine, and the school is closed. Wouldn't Angus come next on your list of 'responsibilities'?"

I can tell she's pissed, but she's trying to keep her voice low because of Stormy. This may be a new trick, I think; if I'm going to piss Cass off, do it while the baby is sleeping.

"No, he isn't. He's fine, and he's working, and I've been... weighing my options," I say.

"That shouldn't take long. Roland, my dead husband, or Angus, alive and breathing and one of the nicest guys on the planet." She reaches for her glass of juice on the coffee table and holds it like she's not sure if she's going to drink it or throw it at me.

"Neither, actually. I'm leaving Deacon." There. I said it. I thought about it all night, about Angus, about my plans before I met him, and this morning, I called the San Diego school district back and set up an interview. Even if I don't get the job there, I know this is what I want to do. I can still go back to school somewhere else. I can walk on the beach. I can start over. I hold my breath, not wanting to drown in the orange juice I think I'm about to get in my face. Instead, she laughs.

"I think you need some of my crazy pills," she says.

"No, I'm thinking clearer than I ever have. You know, the only time I've been really happy in my life was when I was away at college. Even after I had Shaylene and was going to classes and trying to take care of a baby, I was happy. And it wasn't because I was twenty. It was because I was away from here. This town drains me, and now it damn near killed me. I'm not going to let it."

Babe Shatner comes from the kitchen, carrying a covered dish. "I'm taking this to Grace. I left a cobbler in the kitchen for you," she says to Cass as she walks by. She doesn't say squat to me. Cass must have told her about me wanting to break it off with Angus. Fine. I don't need her approval either.

"Since when are your grandmother and Grace Cloud friends?" I ask after she's left, and I shake my head. Everyone in this town, even Babe Shatner, is just trying to get the approval of others. I did it for too long. No more.

"They've been friends for a while now, and if you hadn't noticed, her husband just died. What do you care, anyway? It's all about you, right?"

"Cass—"

"And please tell me of your 'responsibilities.' Tell me you've at least called Grace Cloud to say something about Benny? Or Fat Tina?"

I shake my head. I've been meaning to call them both, but in truth, I don't know what to say. Benny was just doing his job, and I don't think Grace wants me to say that. And Tina, well, after I tell Angus, I doubt she'd even take my call.

"Unbelievable!" she says.

I hear Lola say "Shhh" from the hallway and shut the door to the bedroom and realize that we have been talking a little louder. I don't want to argue with Cass. There's no point.

"Look, I'm sorry you don't understand. I'm sorry I won't be around to help with Stormy, but you'll be fine. And I'm sorry if Angus gets his feelings hurt, but he'll be fine too. But I won't be fine if I stay here and keep doing what I have been doing. Shaylene is at school most of the year, and... I'll figure it out." Just the thought of exploring someplace new, building a life that is not defined by my past, excites me, and it reminds me of when I went away to college all those years ago. And this conversation is very similar to the one I had with Cass then. She's hurt, not because of Angus or because she thinks I'm doing something irrational but because she's going to miss me. "I'm so sorry, Cass."

"You're right. I don't understand, and you are sorry." She gets up and grabs both of our glasses and heads to the kitchen. I take this as my sign that our conversation is over, and even though I hadn't been looking forward to telling her, it's over, and it wasn't as bad as I expected. I know she's upset, but a lot has happened, and she'll warm up to it in the next couple of months before I go. And I'll keep in touch, so it's not like I'm breaking the bond entirely.

I head out the door, careful to shut it quietly so I don't wake the baby.

But there is one tie I do have to break. I pull my phone from my purse and text Angus: *CAN YOU MEET ME AT THE HOUSE?*

He responds almost immediately: *THIRTY MINUTES.*

I step off the porch, and the sun envelops me. I lift my face to it, shut my eyes, and suck in its warmth. Freedom. It feels like freedom.

SHAYLENE IS SITTING in a car that I recognize in front of the house when I pull into the driveway. It belongs to Sammie, the bartender at Tina's, and a friend of Angus's. I pull in the garage and hit the button to close it and, at the last minute, glance back in my rearview and see Shaylene kiss her before getting out of the car. It's just a peck, and even though I know she's a lesbian, I'm not used to seeing it. It's okay. *It's her life. Whatever makes her happy.*

She's coming in through the front door just as I enter from the garage.

"Hey, Mom," she yells as she goes down the hall toward her room. I follow her and lean against the doorjamb, watching her as she digs through her chest of drawers.

"Was that Sammie?" I really don't want to pry, but I do want to see her reaction.

She smiles. A genuine, wide-mouthed Shaylene smile. "Yeah. We've been helping at the mop factory this morning." She peels off her sweatshirt and replaces it with a long-sleeved T-shirt. "I just had to change. It's getting hot out there."

She's a gorgeous girl. Smart. Athletic. Compassionate. It's hard to believe that Roland and I made this perfect woman.

She notices me staring. "What's up?"

"Can I talk to you for a minute?" Shaylene adores Angus, and who wouldn't? I do adore him. I do love him. I just need something more.

She flops down on her bed with one leg under her and pats the bed. "Sure."

She's so easy. Easygoing, easy to please, easy to talk to. She's me at nineteen, without a Roland to complicate things.

"It's about Gus. He'll be here in a minute, and I've made some decisions that are going to be hard." I feel like I'm practicing my Angus speech on Shaylene.

She nods. "I think he sees it coming, Mom. You've been avoiding him."

"Has he said something?" I know Shaylene has been helping all over town, and I know Angus has been trying to run the police station with Benny gone, so I know they've been in contact quite a bit over the past few days.

"He asked how you're doing. He's worried about you."

I suck in a deep breath and let it out slowly. "He shouldn't be. I'm fine."

She cocks her head and looks at me for a minute. "Are you sure? You can tell me, you know. I'm not a kid anymore."

I smile. "No, you aren't. I'm really proud of you for stepping in and helping around town. And yes, I'm fine. I just need to do a few things for myself, things I've never done. And I can't do them if I'm stuck in this town."

She slowly nods. "I get it. Now that I've been in Lawrence, Deacon is a nice place to visit, but—"

"But there's so much more out there." I wrap my arms around her and hug her with everything I have. She hugs me back then breaks free and stands up.

"I gotta go. Sammie's going to take me to see Dad later, so don't expect me home soon. And do me a favor?'

"Anything." And I truly mean anything.

"Try to be nice. Angus is a great guy, but I get it, if he's not for you... Just be nice."

"I am nice! And he's not for me."

"Maybe you should try women?" She laughs and heads down the hall just as the doorbell rings.

"Sorry about the motorcycle," Angus is saying to Shaylene as I round the corner.

I cross my hands over my chest. "What motorcycle?"

"Gus was going to teach me to ride his Harley this summer. But it didn't survive the storm," Shaylene says.

"Well, thank God for small favors," I say. Shaylene has no business on a Harley, and I'm sure they were keeping this little secret from me because they both knew what I would say.

"Easy to replace," Angus says. "By Fourth of July, I'll have you riding my new hog like a champ."

"Sweet!" she says and leans down to kiss Angus on the cheek. He smiles that wonderful smile, and I know that, whatever happens between us, Shaylene and Angus will maintain their friendship. And I'm glad for that. She's right. He's a great guy. *Just not for me.*

"Bye, Mom." She waves to me as she walks out the door.

And then Angus and I are alone.

"Hi," he says.

I nod toward the door. "How's it going out there?" This is already more awkward than I had anticipated. He's going to want an explanation, and I don't have much of one to give him. Sure, I could tell him that I was thinking about this before he came along, and I could tell him about seeing Roland and how I realized I still loved a dead man more than him, and I could tell him that when I think of the future, I see so much more for myself than a house on Booker Hill. But what would be the point?

He shrugs. "Devastation. You want the death count?"

He isn't usually so abrupt or so cold. I write it off as him being tired.

"Not really," I say.

"I didn't think so. Look, Maryanne, we need to talk," he says.

"I know. That's why I called." I turn toward the kitchen, knowing he'll follow, and grab us both a soda from the refrigerator. My mouth is already dry. I set both cans on the table and sit. Angus sits next to me. He opens his soda and takes a long drink. Then he reaches into his pocket and takes out a small square box and lays it on the table. A ring box.

"Angus—"

"Let me talk first, okay?"

"But—"

He holds up a hand. "Maryanne, please. Just listen to me, and then I'll listen to you."

My shoulders slump a little, and I nod. This is going to break his heart, and I can't stop it.

"I've been carrying this around for a week. I was going to give it to you this weekend." He opens the box, and a huge diamond stares back at me. I can't look at him, so I focus on the ring. Then he reaches over, closes the box, and puts it back into his pocket. "But I've changed my mind."

"What?" He's breaking up with me?

"I loved you, Maryanne. Or thought I did. But the last few days... People are out there hurting, they're injured, they are out of places to live and are starting to bury their loved ones. And you don't care. You haven't even bothered to call Tina or Grace, and Benny died saving you. I tell ya, I never saw this side of you."

"You don't understand," I say. This isn't how I saw this going at all. I wasn't prepared to be put on the defensive, and I don't particularly like it.

He shakes his head. "I don't need to understand. All I know is, I can't see myself spending the rest of my life with someone who is so horribly selfish. I'm sorry." He drinks the rest of his soda while I sit speechless. Then he jumps off the chair with a wave over his head and struts to the door.

He broke up with me? Selfish? The little bastard.

I stand up, pick up the soda can, and throw it as hard as possible and hit him in the back of the head. He turns around, and I stand with my legs apart, my hands on my hips, ready for a fight. But he smiles, which pisses me off more, and snaps his fingers like he forgot something.

"Oh yeah," he says, "thanks for the soda."

Chapter 24
Clay

I *am blessed.*

I only have to walk a few feet, but even when I'm using the handrails, it hurts like hell. A broken hip ain't for sissies, that's for sure, and the added bonus of a lower leg cast makes it even more challenging. I'm drenched in sweat and know when I take this next step, it's going to feel like fire shooting through my groin. I have to do it—it's the only way I'm going to ever get back to walking on my own again—and it starts here. But I don't have to like it.

"Grr." I sound like an old bear.

"You're doing good. You're almost there, and then you can rest." The therapist is young and not a very big woman, but she has arms of steel and assures me that if I fall, she'll catch me. I'm a pretty big guy, and I don't think I'd bet on her winning that match, but I don't intend to find out. Her name is Kendra, and even though she talks very nice, she's also a bit of a drill sergeant and makes sure I know she's in charge.

Another step and I'm to the end, and Kendra has the wheelchair behind me and helps me lower myself into it. It still hurts but is a little better now that she's put an extra cushion on it.

"That's it for this morning, Mr. Adams. We'll do it again this afternoon. I promise it will get easier, but it's not going to happen overnight." She hands me a towel to wipe my face, and a bottle of cold water.

"Clay," I say as I open the bottle and down it in two gulps. "If I call you Kendra, then you call me Clay." If I'm going to let her torture me, I might as well be on a more personal level with her about it.

"Clay." She takes the empty bottle from me and hands me a fresh one. She props the right leg of the wheelchair up so my foot is pointed out front. "Remember to keep it up if you can. It will help with the swelling."

The place I'm in has been open less than a year, and as far as rehab facilities go, I guess it's a good one. I'm trying not to call it a nursing home, but that's what it seems like to me. I know everyone here is supposed to be on the mend, but most are pretty old and I think have been here for a while. The carpet is a blue-green, the walls have flowery wallpaper, and the cafeteria is actually six smaller rooms, each with a large dining table and heavy wooden chairs, all of it meant to make you feel "at home." It ain't working.

"When can I get out of here?" I ask.

"It depends. You'll need to do therapy every day for a while, and if you don't have a good support system, someone who can bring you here and will make sure you follow the rules at home, it's best that you stay." She wheels me into my room and opens the blinds on my windows, letting the sun in.

"My wife just had a baby," I say. "And I've got plenty of help at home."

"I'll do my best," she says.

In other words, she has no idea and isn't about to commit to a timeline.

I tell her I'm going to sit up for a while because I don't want to get in the habit of lying in bed all day. Cass won't be here until the afternoon, so I decide to make a few calls and check on the house.

My homeowners insurance is on the ball, and I make an appointment for Cass to meet them tomorrow afternoon. It means I won't get my daily visit, but we've got to start getting things back to normal. I have a family now, and I want them in our home. Just thinking about Cass and Stormy makes the pain better. Regardless of the shape I'm in, I feel truly blessed.

I decide to call Tina at the club and tell her thank you. But then I remember that Tina's club was smashed, and I don't have her cell number. I know Angus will have it, and I'll be able to check on Cass through him as well. She says everything's fine, but I'd like another opinion. Just checking. It's kind of my job.

Angus answers on the first ring, and I can tell from his voice he's tired. He's usually very upbeat, and you can hear him talking through a big smile, but this morning, his voice is softer and slower. "Are you done at the resort and ready to get back here to help?" he asks.

"I wish. Sorry I haven't called. I've been drugged up and a little preoccupied," I say.

"Shaylene's kept me informed. That's a great kid you got there. She's doing double the work of some of the men in this town."

I smile. She is something. And I've got two great girls now.

"How's Maryanne?" I ask.

He makes a sound like a mumbled growl. "Well, you'd have to ask her. I broke it off. I figured Cass would have told you about it."

Oh shit.

"Sorry, Angus. I didn't know." Maryanne is the mother of my oldest child, and I hate to bad-mouth her, but honestly, she's not what I would consider wife material for anyone. I think being with Angus for the past six or seven months is the longest she's ever been faithful, and I wouldn't bet the house on that.

"I've got more important things to worry about right now," he says, "like a buffalo to return to the Quapaw tribe."

I understand the tough-guy mentality—I pretty much own it. And he may say it's all good, but I know he's hurting. He loved Maryanne, I could tell, and it's never that easy. *Did he say a buffalo?*

"Well, if you want to talk about it, or get drunk and cuss about it, give me a few weeks, okay?"

"I'll keep that invitation in mind."

"How's Cass?" I know he's been to Babe's house every day since the tornado. Cass is his employee and his friend, and Angus isn't the type of guy to not make sure his people are looked after.

"Unemployed. And happier than I've ever seen her."

I smile. Yeah, she's been on top of the world since Stormy came along. "Angus, I need to call Tina, and I don't have a number for her."

"I'll text it to your phone. You may have to try a few times. She doesn't pick up often. She's having a rough time with Benny and all," he says.

Tina has always seemed so tough to me, and from what I hear about her riding out the tornado in her bar, digging Daze and Pet out from their house, and doing all she did for me, Maryanne, and even Benny, it kind of surprises me that she's not handling it all well. I guess we all have a breaking point, and I feel even worse that I haven't called her before now.

"I hate to hear that," I say. "If there's anything I can do..."

"Give her a call. And get well. We could use you right now."

I hang up and wait for Angus's text and immediately call Tina. It goes straight to voicemail. "Tina, this is Clay Adams. I don't know when I'm getting out of here, and I really want to talk to you and thank you for everything. Please give me a call."

As I hit End on my phone, one of the nurses pokes her head in my door. "You have a visitor," she says.

I look at the clock on the wall—ten thirty, way too early for Cass.

"Hello, Clay."

It's Grace Cloud, and suddenly I feel like shit for not calling her. It's not that Benny and I were close. We were once, but years changed that. For the most part, we got along, even if he did throw me in jail last year. He was just doing his job, I know, but he seemed to like to pick on

Cass, and I was never okay with that. But all that doesn't really matter. A man dies, you call his wife.

"Grace." I hold up the phone in my hand. "I was going to call you. I'm so sorry about Benny." I am sorry. Benny was my age, forty-one, and way too young to die. "You didn't have to come."

Grace is a pretty woman: blond, petite, and always looks… clean. I don't know any other way to say it. She doesn't wear a lot of makeup, just enough to have some color, and her hair is always shiny and smooth but not like she's been to a fancy place to get it done. She's wearing a pair of blue jeans and a Fleetwood Mac T-shirt, and if I didn't know better, I'd think she was just running errands.

She looks around my room. "I wanted to come. I heard you were hurt pretty bad, and to be honest, I needed to get out of the house. Too many memories in there right now." She gives me a weak smile, and I can't help but admire her. "You want to go outside?"

"I'd love to, but they won't let me out yet without someone on staff to escort me. They got me pumped up with painkillers, and I figure they think I'll try to escape."

She gets behind my wheelchair and unlocks the brakes. "I used to work with the head nurse. It'll be fine."

As we go down the hall toward the courtyard, we pass the nurses' station, and one of the nurses nods to Grace. It's that simple. I respect the woman even more now.

She wheels me to a quiet corner in the shade and parks me next to a bench. It's a beautiful morning, and the breeze feels good on my skin. It may not seem like much, but I'm an outdoor kind of guy, and this is better than getting an extra Jell-O at dinner.

"Did you know that Benny and I joined the army together on the Buddy Program?" I ask. Now that she's sitting here, I'm thinking back and trying to remember good times with Benny.

"Yes," she says. "He told me you were very close as kids."

"Our dads were friends, so we were forced together at an early age. After mine left town, Tenesy would come check on us, and in school, Benny and I just naturally hung together."

"I can't imagine Tenesy being young and... nice." She shakes her head. "He's always been nice to me, but he and Benny had a difficult relationship. And yet he checked on your mother and you boys. Good for him."

"Well, him and Rudy Drown."

She looks at me and literally bites her lip. I start laughing. "I'll say it for us both. With Freddy Adams, Tenesy Cloud, and Rudy Drown as our male role models, it's pretty amazing that Benny and I turned out to be good men."

"But you both did," she says and raises her hand like she's toasting us. I do the same and we clink our imaginary glasses.

"I wish things had gone different, Grace. I guess you just never know." I'm not real good at this stuff. I hope she doesn't start crying.

She takes a deep breath. "Benny had some health issues, and we were trying to work them through. I guess that and the stress of the day... I'm sad, horribly sad, but I've been a cop's wife for a long time, and it's always in the back of your mind. Several years ago, when we first moved to Deacon, Benny got shot in the arm when he jumped in front of a man trying to kill his wife."

"Stevie Walker. I remember that."

"Yes, that was his name. I was frantic. His left upper arm, six inches from his heart. It healed quickly, but it was so close. Benny told me, 'I couldn't let him just kill her. And if he'd killed me instead, at least I would have saved her.' And that was supposed to make me feel better." She smiles and looks at her lap for a minute. "I guess, in time, that's what will give me some peace. He didn't exactly jump in front of a bullet, but he died while trying to save someone else, no matter which version of the story flying around town you believe. And he wouldn't have had it any other way."

Cass had told me about Maryanne's story, which was quickly snuffed by what Tina Early told Angus. I think at the time, she wanted me to verify one or the other, since I was there, and I kind of think that's what Grace is doing right now too. But the truth is, I don't know. I was flat on my back and had no idea what was going on upstream.

"Have you talked to Tina?" I ask.

"Not really." She leaves it at that. I think about making excuses for Tina, after talking to Angus this morning, but that's not what she came here for. I know what she came for.

"Grace, I wish I could tell you what really happened, but I can't. I was pretty shook up, and I have no idea. But you're right, it doesn't matter. Benny would have laid down his life for anyone. Tina's the only one who was present for the entire scene, so if I were to believe anyone, it would be her." And in Tina's version, Benny is a real hero.

She nods and smiles. "Thank you, Clay." Then she reaches for my hand, and I take it. Like two old friends.

Yes, Benny and I joined the army together twenty-two years ago on the Buddy Program. A lot of shit happened between then and now, and we both came back different men. But at the time, we promised to look out for each other. I never really understood what that meant until now.

I got your back, buddy.

Chapter 25

Cass

"**Y**ou have got to be kidding me!"

It's been six days since I had Stormy, and that means six nights since I've had any peace whatsoever. Sure, Stormy keeps me up, but I don't mind that. It's Lola. And Grams. And Maryanne. And Angus. And Shaylene. And tomorrow, Clay comes home from the rehab facility, and I'm sure he'll be another one to keep me from getting any rest whatsoever. So tonight, I borrowed Grams's car, left Stormy with my army of babysitter-family members, and drove down to the river to find a little quiet. And of course, there stands Benny Cloud, as if he were waiting for me.

He shrugs, as if I should have expected it.

"Doesn't anybody just die and go to heaven anymore?" Or hell, or wherever they're supposed to go?

He places his thumb and forefinger together like he's pinching something, taps it on his chest, then points at his eyes. I have no idea what that means.

"Well, I guess this at least answers the question of whether I can still see dead people." I plop down on the grass and cross my legs, looking out across the river. Benny sits next to me as if we're two old friends passing the time.

"Sorry you're dead, Benny."

He nods. I guess I should be thankful that he ain't talking.

I figure it doesn't hurt to be nice to the guy now that he's dead. It's not like he'll ever be arresting me again. "And thanks for doing what you did. Not the dying part, but the helping Clay and saving Maryanne part. Fat Tina told everybody what you did."

He shakes his head, and I have no idea what that means.

I don't get it. I figured when you die, someone comes for you to lead you where you're supposed to go. Or there's some path you know to take. Or like some people say, there's a light and you just know to follow it. Maryanne said Roland came for her. Even though she turned him down like a bedsheet. But nobody came for Benny?

He shakes his head like he's read my mind and points across the river. There's a grove of trees I can barely see silhouetted against the night sky and a bright light in the center. The light shines on the water, a bridge of light that comes all the way across to the other side. I always knew Benny wasn't the sharpest knife in the drawer, but the path he needs to take seems pretty obvious to me.

"Ta da!" I wave my hand toward it. Surely this isn't the reason I see dead people: to show the dumb ones which way to go. He shakes his head and taps his fingers to his chest, harder this time.

"It looks real nice over there, Benny. Surely you know some people over there you want to see. How about that Jimmy kid? Or maybe Roland?"

He throws his head back and opens his mouth wide, like he's laughing. *Yeah, you're right, where Roland is probably isn't that pretty.* I sigh deeply.

"Look, Benny. This walking the shores bit can't be much fun. Especially considering I'm the only one that can see you and we ain't that good of friends. And I won't be coming down here a lot to keep you company. I can't. I have Clay and Stormy—"

He smiles real big and nods when I mention the baby.

"Thank you," I say.

I look toward the trees again. Roland didn't have a pretty bridge, but why would he? But neither did Old Man Booker, who I used to see when I lived on the Hill. Of course, he'd been dead for many years by then, so maybe... "Benny, you need to go. I have a bad feeling that you don't get to wait forever."

He crosses his arms over his chest and shakes his head. Even in death, he's hardheaded.

"What happens if you wait too long? What if you're stuck here?" I'm starting to feel a little anxious. I know it's not my responsibility to point out the obvious, but I *am* the only one who can see him.

He looks at me with hollow eyes and slowly shakes his head.

We sit there for a good five minutes, just looking out over the water. The little light bridge changes colors, from yellow, to pink, to violet, to blue, and it's so pretty, I almost want to check it out myself. But I can't. And there's nothing I can do for Benny. I stand up and brush the grass from my behind. "I gotta go, Benny. Your funeral is tomorrow, and I promised Clay I'd be there with him. Please go across the bridge, Benny. There's nothing here for you."

He shakes his head slowly and, one more time, taps his chest.

I shake my head back at him and, one more time, point at the bridge.

Chapter 26
Tina

It's been a week since the tornado, and it seems like yesterday. I haven't been able to sleep, and without having the club as a distraction, all I do is think about everything that happened. It was horrible—from the minute that thing dropped on my club, to seeing the town of Deacon looking like a scene from a war zone, to Maryanne and Benny.

It's nine o'clock, Harley just got back from town, and I'm sitting on the couch in my housecoat, petting Velvet. Harley has a bag from one of those fast-food places in Deacon and sits it on the dining room table then comes and takes my hand. "Let's eat," he says, "then we got to start getting ready."

I shake my head. "I don't think I can do it. What am I going to say to Grace?" Today is Benny's funeral. Actually, Jimmy's funeral then Benny's funeral. Back to back. A doubleheader. But Jimmy's mother has chosen to have a small private service with family only, which means I have to sit through just one.

Harley gets the bag of food off the table and sits by me on the couch. He pushes Velvet off my lap and hands me a bacon-and-egg biscuit. I open it and take a bite. Tasteless.

"You're going to tell her exactly what you've been telling everyone else. Benny dragged that woman out of the water. He's the one that Heimliched her. Then while you were tending to her, he had a heart attack and died. And then you are going to hug her and tell her we will do whatever we can to help her, and we will."

It's a convenient lie. Harley doesn't believe it—I can tell by the way he pushes his eyebrows together when I say it—but he's not questioning me. He knows I have my reasons. He thinks I'm just honoring Benny by making him sound like a hero, which in a way, I am. He is a hero. The last thing he did in this life was to try to save someone else, even when he was dying himself. But there's another reason I can't tell anyone the truth, and it is completely selfish.

Even though Benny told me to get Maryanne, I'm a grown woman, and in that instant, I had to make a choice: try to save my friend or help a woman I don't exactly care for because my friend requested it. I made the choice. And with every choice, there are consequences. People die, people live, people hurt, people rejoice. The names change with the choices we make. Considering that Benny is dead and Maryanne isn't, I think I made the wrong one.

"I saw Angus in town, and he's doing fine. Looks mighty tired, but he's handling everything like a man," Harley says. I know that "everything" includes all the work he's been doing trying to help the people of Deacon, as well as the fact that he broke it off with Maryanne before she had a chance to do it to him. He says he doesn't have time to worry about some woman, but I know he loved her, and I know he's hurting. We all hide things, but it's hard to hide them from ourselves.

Harley takes the empty wrapper from my hands. I hadn't realized I ate the entire biscuit. "Now, let's get in the shower and get ready. I know it's going to be a hard day, but I'll be with you every step. You can do this, Tina. *We* can do this."

I let him help me up then let him help me shower. Once we're both dressed, Harley gets me in the Hummer, and we drive into Deacon to the Second Baptist Church. People are piling in, and I don't want to move.

"How are you feeling?" Harley asks as he puts the Hummer in park.

I take a deep breath and nod. But it's just another lie.

Numb. I feel numb.

Sammie and Sonja saved us a spot on the back pew, and I'm thankful for that. I try my best to shrink into the pew so I'm not noticed, which is kind of hard for me to do. But it doesn't keep the others who enter from leaning over from behind me to tell me thank you, or sorry about the club, or some other trite greeting meant to make *them* feel better, not me.

"Say, there, Tina. Good to see you in town again." It's Daze Harper, and I turn slightly to see that his brother, Pet, is with him. I'm sure Beth is here, too, but other than the day of the tornado, when I thought she had suddenly become my "friend" of sorts, she hasn't come to the house or called or anything. Figures. When someone needs you, they love you. But when the disaster is over, it's the same old crap. I'm sure if my club were still standing, she'd be out there picketing it by now.

"Thanks, Daze. Pet. I'm sorry I haven't been much help. I can't seem to..."

What? I can't seem to get my shit together?

"I know this might be a little early, but are you planning on rebuilding the club?" Pet asks. I don't see Pet much, and he doesn't frequent my club like his brother, but he's always been nice when I have seen him.

"Oh, I don't... I haven't really thought about it." I was well insured, and I'm sure rebuilding it would be the thing to do, but maybe I could use the money to do something else with my life? I just don't know.

"Well, if you do, Daze and I are willin' to help. Shoot, I bet we could get twenty guys to help put it back up. It'd be like a barn raisin'. Hey! A 'bar raisin'!" Pet snickers at his own play on words, and the sound of laughter, even Pet's, seems foreign to me at a funeral.

"Yeah, and that would sure piss Beth off," Daze says. Which makes it all the better in Daze's mind.

I shake my head and feel my face crack in a little smile.

Harley pats my knee and whispers in my ear. "Good to see a smile again."

People are pouring in to pay their last respects to Benny. He grew up in Deacon and served his community well. Because he was an active police chief, almost every county in Kansas sent a representative to parade his body to the cemetery. I didn't even realize they do that. Benny would be amazed at the turnout. I see the undersheriff, Darnell Dix, sitting with the mayor, but no Rudy Drown. What an ass.

I hear Cass Adams and turn to see her pushing Clay in a wheelchair, with Lola, Babe Shatner, and Shaylene close behind. No Maryanne Spencer, thank God. I don't want to see her or talk to her or think about her. Clay's right leg is casted and propped up to stick straight out in front of him. He left a few messages for me this week, and now I feel bad that I didn't call him back. I just didn't want to talk. "Can we scoot in here?" Lola asks Harley. She points at Clay. "He can't really get in the pew."

Harley says sure, and we all start moving down. Lola, Babe Shatner, and Shaylene go around the back of the pew and get in next to Sonja and Sammie. Cass sits next to Harley, with Clay on the end in the aisle. It doesn't take him long to start talking.

"Tina, if you need anything, just ask."

Cass cackles. "Like you could do anything right now, anyway." She turns to me and says, "That's his way of saying thank you. He says he owes you one. I told him you'd probably be happier with one of his spice cakes, but he says that isn't enough."

I don't see Cass much, but I've known her all my life. One thing I've always noticed about her is how curious her eyes are. The pupil is like a sunken pit of darkness in the center of a dull green pool. Haunting. Dismal. Sad. Today, though, they shine and sparkle like green stars. Her hair hangs light and loose around her face, and her smile, which was always a little chilling, now seems mischievous, playful. She's wearing a lemon-yellow sundress, and that alone makes her stand out in the sea of funeral black. But she looks absolutely stunning. And I never thought I'd say that about Cass Adams. She seems happy.

And her boobs are huge!

She notices me looking at her chest and straightens her shoulders and wiggles her eyebrows at me. I almost laugh out loud but remember where I am. "Motherhood has done you well," I say. "I bet she's a beauty."

She's digging in her purse and pulls out her cell phone. Leaning over Harley, she starts flipping through her gallery. "Here she is. And again. And here she is with Grams. And—"

A sudden hush falls over the chapel, and we both turn from the phone to see Benny's mother, Josie, accompanied by a skinny older man. It takes me a moment to recognize him as Tenesy. Grace walks in behind them, and my heart aches. She stands with her head held high and a permanent smile that looks like it's Xanax induced. She nods to several people, places a hand on Clay's shoulder, and whispers something in his ear. He nods and squeezes her hand. When she turns, she notices me, and her smile seems to waver, or maybe I just imagine it. She makes her way behind the pew so she's directly behind me.

I turn to her, and I can see the pain in her eyes. She wraps her arms around my neck and hugs me from behind. "Thank you, Tina. I'm glad you were with him. He thought the world of you, and I know you did all you could do for him."

I lean on Harley, who puts his arm around me, and I cry pools of tears, not even trying to hold it in.

Harley and Angus say I saw too much in one day and it might take some time for me to be able to process it all. They both have had traumatic experiences, and I'm sure they know all about that sort of thing, but it isn't just the fact that I saw so much loss and devastation. I made choices on that day. Choices that I will have to live with for the rest of my life.

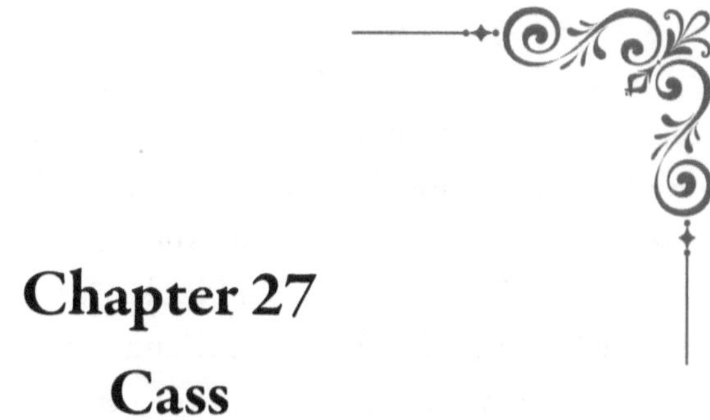

Chapter 27

Cass

Funerals are funny things. When people die, a bunch of other people get together in a little chapel and listen to sad music and a preacher telling us all about heaven. All this time, the dead person is lying up front in a casket so the audience gets one last look at him. It's like an encore at a concert but without having to light our lighters. I think most people listen to the music and the preacher and try to convince themselves that the dead guy is going to a better place, but it's mostly for them, to make them feel better. I focus on the body, hoping he'll suddenly open his eyes and thinking how everybody would freak out if he did.

The only part of a funeral that really makes much sense to me is the end, when everybody lines up and walks past the body and says goodbye. Again, it's for them, because I don't think Benny can hear them, but it seems more fitting. You're going away, and we're saying goodbye. That makes sense.

We're on the back row, so we go first in line. I push Clay up the center aisle, and all eyes are on us and Tina behind us. I know everybody's heard the story of what happened, even though I'm not convinced Tina's version of Benny saving Maryanne then falling down after is very believable. Maryanne said she didn't even see Benny when she was out on that tree trunk, only Tina moving toward her. But I guess it doesn't really matter. He's dead either way.

Clay says goodbye to Benny, and I lean close and whisper, "Cross the bridge." Tina is behind me, blubbering on her husband, and I'm ready to get moving back to my row and get this over with. I left Stormy with Maryanne, and I don't know what kind of crap she's going to try to teach her before I get home. And besides, if I want to talk to Benny, I know where to find him. I look over at his wife, Grace, and give her a little smile. Not that we're friends or anything, but I remember at Roland's funeral, she was one of the only people who was nice to me. She smiles back. She seems like a nice woman. I don't know what she saw in Benny.

Angus is behind her with the other guys who worked with Benny, and I wink at him as we pass. He looks like he's been on a two-day drunk, but I know it's because he's been trying to put Deacon back together. And of course, get over Maryanne. I feel bad for him, but I know he deserves better anyway. She'll leave, he'll move on, and in the long run, he'll be better off.

I'm going to miss her too. It's been nice having a friend for the past year. All those years with Roland, I always wanted a girlfriend, but it seemed like after he was gone, Maryanne and I connected because she *needed* one. I was pissed when she first told me she was leaving town, but maybe I'll be better off when she's gone too. She's a constant reminder of Roland, and now that Clay and I have started a family, I want to put him behind me forever. He'll always be a part of me, I can't help that, but sometimes, seeing Maryanne brings back things I'd rather keep tucked away.

But I didn't want her dead. That's the thing that keeps coming back to me. I was so worried, enough that I asked Clay to watch out for her. Sure, Clay is Clay, and he would have probably done the same thing he did no matter what I asked of him, but maybe there was a trade-off in this whole seeing-visions thing that I wasn't aware of? Maybe she lived, but Clay had to get hurt in the process because I interfered? Or was Benny the cost of keeping her alive? Maybe I feel like she owes somebody something, but she'll never know that, because I can't tell her about my visions. I don't trust her enough to share that.

Clay and I are sitting on the back row, waiting for it to be over, and even though I know it's polite to let everyone get through their good-byes, I'm antsy and want to leave. I decide to look through my Stormy pictures while the parade before the casket continues.

I can't help but smile when I look at her. I was so scared before I had her, wondered if I was even sane enough to take care of a baby and, even worse, worried whether she'd be normal. But she's perfect. I'd heard people say that when you have a kid, you change, and I always thought that was kind of silly. I mean, the only thing that really changes is now you have another mouth to feed and you have to watch the kid to make sure it doesn't run off or eat shoe polish. But now I know what they meant. I love Clay, I love Grams, and I love Lola. But I would do anything, and I mean *anything*, for Stormy. It's like all these years, I had a little empty space in my heart, and she not only fills it but makes it overflow. I figure that's why I can't stop smiling.

Clay nudges me, and I look up from my phone and see that Benny's mom and dad are in front of his casket now, so only his wife is left. I put my phone away and wait. When she gets up there, she seems to be talking to his body, but I can't hear what she's saying. Then she does something that I don't expect.

She pinches two fingers together, taps her chest, then points at her eyes.

"Did you see that?" I ask Clay, and he looks at me and shrugs like he doesn't know what I'm talking about. I turn to Tina instead. "That little thing she did with her hands, did you see that?"

Tina looks at me with her face all red and scrunched up and shakes her head. Her bottom lip is quivering, and I hope she doesn't start crying again. I look down the row at Lola and Grams, and Grams is staring right at me. I turn back toward the front and don't say anything more.

"You ready?" Clay asks.

People are starting to leave, and although I want to get back home, I need to find out about that hand motion. It seems to be the only thing Benny is going to say to me, so I'd like to at least know what the hell it means. And I guess Grace Cloud is the only one who can tell me.

"Not just yet," I say as I stand up and squeeze past his extended leg in the wheelchair. I head to the front of the church, and Angus sees me and is by my side before I get to Grace.

"What are you doing, Cass?" He looks concerned, like he's going to grab me and drag me out if I do something stupid, but I wave him off.

I walk right in the middle of a gaggle of women talking to Grace and cut them all off. "Can I ask you something?"

Everyone around goes dumb, like they fully expect me to say something awful. Angus is shaking his head at me, telling me to stop. I guess my reputation precedes me.

But Grace gives me a warm smile. "Of course."

"That little hand thing you did at Benny's casket. I saw him do it last night. I mean, last week. What does it mean?"

"You mean this?" She taps her fingers on her chest and points at her eyes.

"Yes! That."

"It's just something Benny and I used to do. It means I love you and I'll see you soon," she says.

I smile so wide that I think my face is going to crack, and she looks at me like I've lost my mind. But I'm used to that. I almost skip down the aisle toward Clay.

I know what Benny wants and how to get him to cross that bridge.

LOLA WENT BACK TO SPRINGFIELD right after the funeral, so when we got back to the house, I sent Maryanne on her way and put Clay and Stormy to bed so I could have a long talk with Grams. I told her everything about me seeing dead people. She wasn't shocked or upset. It's kind of like she knew in a way and was just waiting for me to say it.

"I always knew you had a gift," she said.

I always figured "a gift" was something that you used to help people, not something that haunts you. Seeing Roland and Old Man Booker and even Mama Adams, I thought they were there to make my life miserable. But maybe not. Maybe they all needed something, and I'm the only one who could give it to them. I don't know what it could be, but with Benny, I know.

He won't cross that bridge until he sees Grace again. And I'm the only one who can make that happen.

Grams and I are sitting in the kitchen, our normal spot for "serious" conversations, and drinking sweet tea. "The bridge you saw, tell me more about it," she says.

"I don't know how to explain it. It was... amazing. There were colors that I don't think I've ever seen before, every color, all at once. Shining, almost like the lights and colors were singing. When I looked at it, it was everything beautiful I've ever known, and things I can't even imagine, all spread out on a shiny platter." I shake my head. *It was so much more, but I can't put it into words.*

Grams nods. "And it was obviously there for Benny?"

"Yes. Definitely. He pointed at the trees, and it came right toward him."

Grams squeezes my hands. "People who have died and come back have talked about things: lights at the end of tunnels, open doors, bridges. I guess it's the way they go to whatever is next."

"What if they don't?" I ask. I've thought about that, too. I've figured out that Benny wants to see Grace, and maybe that will be enough for him to go away, but I have to tell Grace my secret to do that. And I'm not sure if it's worth it.

"Well, I wish I knew. But I can't imagine that a bridge as beautiful as you describe is there for no reason. If he wasn't meant to cross it..."

I nod. "I have to tell Grace."

"Are you sure you want to do this?" Grams asks. She's skeptical, because she knows me so well. The truth is, I never really cared much for many people, and the idea of me helping someone out of the kindness of my heart kind of throws me for a loop too. But when I look at Stormy, I want to be a better person.

I shake my head. "Not at all. I don't want this, Grams, this 'gift.' But this is the only way I can make Benny go away. I have Clay, and now I have Stormy, and I just want to be... normal." There. I said it. I've always thought it, but to be honest, I haven't really thought it was possible. From the time I saw my momma hanging in the closet when I was five, I knew things would never be normal for me. But I tried. With Roland, I wanted the white picket fence, then he moved me out to the Hill. I wanted a baby, but he made sure that never happened. I wanted friends, but the only one I ever had was too busy trying to take my husband to worry about all the drugs he was pumping me up with to make me think I was crazier than I was.

But now with Clay, and Stormy, and our perfect little house, it's right there. That brass ring on the carousel. But as always, it's just out of reach.

"Normal?" She says it like it tastes bad. "What's so great about normal?"

"Seriously, Grams? I understand, be your own person, don't worry about what others think, but I'd just like to not have issues. Things that make me feel damaged." I look down at my hands. I can't look her in the eye right now. I know Grams is special, and I'm not saying it's a bad thing. She's Grams, and I love her, but I don't want to *be* her.

She nods. "Okay, so, tell me, how many normal people do you know?"

I have to think for a minute, because I don't really know many people at all.

"Angus," I say.

"Less than one percent of the people in the world are dwarfs, and less than one percent of the people in the world have an IQ as high as Angus King. Do you know how rare of a human being that makes him?"

"That's different. I mean—"

"Who else?" she asks.

"Fine. Harvey Cox." I have no idea why he came to mind.

"He has four testicles. Next." And now I wish he hadn't come to mind.

I try to think of the most normal person I can think of. "Grace Cloud."

I smile when Grams doesn't come back with something right away.

"I'm not going to share Grace's secrets," she says. I raise an eyebrow, and Grams shakes her head.

"Fine, but I bet she doesn't talk to dead people! Nobody does that," I say.

"Not true, and you know it. A lot of children do, and there are plenty of books about it."

I let out a long sigh.

Grams puts her hand on mine. "Honey, we all have something. And usually, we don't get to choose. We call some good, and we call some bad, but I bet there are a lot of people that would prefer your 'abnormal' over theirs. But it just doesn't work that way. You accept yourself, and then you can be—what's that word again?"

"Normal," I say, smiling.

"Yes."

"So you think I should tell Grace? Try to get her to go to the park with me?"

She shrugs. "You need to do what you think is best for you. Once you tell her, your secret isn't yours anymore."

"But maybe that's the key. Maybe the problem is that I've kept it to myself for so long that I can't be myself. I don't want her to laugh at me. I'm scared." I'm being more honest with Grams than I've ever been, and it feels good, but it's also terrifying.

"Grace is a good and wise woman. I doubt she'll laugh at you. Do you want me to go with you?"

"No. I need to do it by myself. And I'd feel better knowing you were here with Clay and Stormy." *In case Grace decides to have me committed and I don't come home for a while.*

She grabs her purse off the chair next to her and hands me her car keys.

I smile and nod. I can do this. I need to do this.

"Grams? Can I ask you one more thing?"

"Of course, honey. Anything," she says.

"How do you know how many testicles Harvey Cox has?"

THERE WERE A FEW CARS in front of her house, so I drive around town waiting for them to leave. I see a lot of pictures on the TV of those places overseas where a bomb was dropped right in the middle of town, wiping off faces of buildings, most of them just a pile of crap floating into the street. When I look around the neighborhoods, it kind of reminds me of that, except every fourth house is still standing, some with just a wall missing or a few windows broken out, but most flat on the ground.

Deacon will never be the same.

The last car leaves Grace's house around eight o'clock, which is perfect. I'm parked and on her doorstep before their taillights disappear.

"Oh," she says when she sees me at the door. She hesitates for only a minute then invites me in.

The house is not much bigger than my and Clay's, a small living room and dining area with a kitchen and, I figure, a couple of bedrooms down the hall. Casserole dishes and plates line the table, like she just had a potluck party but everyone left their crap for the hostess to clean up. But the thing that really catches my eye is all the damn dolls. Porcelain dolls, some still in boxes, sit on shelves, cabinets, tables, just about anywhere there seems to be a space for them. "Wow," I say.

"Benny knew all their names," Grace says.

"These are *his* dolls?" I smile. I wish I had known he collected dolls when he was alive. I would have definitely had fun with that. One on the mantel catches my eye: blond curly hair, blue eyes, barefoot, wearing a blue jumper with one shoulder undone. She looks ornery. I run my finger over her cold porcelain toes. "This one reminds me of Stormy."

Grace nods. "Babe can't stop talking about the baby. I'm sorry I haven't had time to... Stormy is a beautiful name."

I reach for my phone in my pocket then think this probably isn't the best time to be showing pictures.

Her eyes are red, and she has dark circles under them, and I feel sorry for her. She looks tired, and here I am, keeping her from whatever she's trying to do. Grams was right. This isn't going to be easy.

"Grams baked you a cherry cobbler. But I forgot to bring it." I'm not comfortable around most people. In fact, there are very few I even like to talk to, and I've already had a longer conversation with Grace—a nice one—than I've had with anyone in a long time. I'm starting to sweat a little, and it just feels weird, and the way she's standing there, I can tell she thinks it's weird too. I take a deep breath. It's about to get weirder.

"Can I talk to you about Benny? I need to tell you something, and I don't want you to think I'm crazy. Well, I'm sure you already do, but—" Damn. This wasn't going the way I had practiced in the car on the way over.

"I don't think you're crazy." She motions toward the couch, and I sit with her but keep a distance between us. There's a box on the coffee table, and it's wrapped in gold with a big red bow. She notices me looking at it and smiles. "It was... The night Benny died... The last time I talked to him, I told him I had a surprise for him, and he promised he wouldn't miss it, no matter what. I can't seem to put it away." She fingers the bow on the top of the box.

"Another doll?" I ask.

"Something like that. You said you wanted to tell me something about Benny?" She doesn't seem anxious or pissed that I just showed up at her door and now am being so weird, and I know I would be if I were her. She seems really calm about the whole thing, and I wonder if she's been popping some of the pills my doctor usually gives me. I kind of hope so.

"I went down to the river last night. To the park. And..." I shut my eyes. *Just say it!*

I can't do this.

I shake my head and stand up, but she catches my arm. "And he was there," she says.

She's not asking, she says it like she knows. She knows! I wonder if Angus... I don't care how, but she knows, and she isn't freaking out. I nod and sit back down closer to her and spill everything. "Yes! He's there. And there's this pretty bridge of light, and he won't cross it, and he told me he wanted to see you, well, didn't tell me, but I know that's what he means. I think if you go down there with me, he can see you, and then he'll cross the bridge, and then—"

She moves back a little bit. "I meant you felt his presence, not he was actually there."

Damn. I misread that one. Now she looks scared.

This was a mistake. I get up and move quickly toward the door, but her voice stops me before I can get it open.

"Wait."

I turn, and she's standing, her arms folded across her chest as if she's holding herself. "I..." She shakes her head and reaches for the wrapped box on the table. "You're right. I do think you're crazy. But I'd like to go to the river, and I don't really want to go by myself."

I don't know much about Grace, but I do know quite a bit about crazy. And if she thinks I'm an egg shy of a dozen, then she's got to be a little touched herself if she's going to get in a car with me, at night, and go to the river where her husband died. She could just be on some really good drugs, and I'm all for that. Either way, she's in Grams's car with her seat belt on before I can even get my door open.

I weave the car through the residential neighborhood and find my way to the main drag. There's construction going on, even at night, and we don't say much until we're on Twelfth Street, heading toward Beecher Park at the river. It's too quiet in the car, and it's not like she's going to jump out while I'm driving, so I figure I might as well talk.

"So, you believe me?" I know Grace works on the psych ward at the hospital, and she has experience with people who do strange things, so it wouldn't be too far of a stretch for someone to see dead people. Right?

She smiles and shakes her head. "Absolutely not."

Now I'm really confused. "Then why are you going with me?" I really don't get it.

She has her gift box on her lap, and she's holding it like it might fly away if she takes her hands off it. She looks straight ahead, watching the road, and takes a deep breath. "I believe that sometimes, when people die, their bodies let off so much of the energy that was in them that sometimes, certain people, sensitive people, can still feel it for a while after they are gone. So, when you're there, where they died, you can still feel them, as if they are there."

I look at her and wish I could turn on the inside dome light to see her face. She sure sounds serious. "Then why can I see them?" I ask.

"You can't," she says. "You feel them around you, and your mind creates a vision of the person so it makes sense to you."

"Hmm. So if you don't believe me, if you think it's just 'energy' hanging around in the park, why are you going with me?"

She shrugs. "Because even though he isn't really there, it feels like he is. And I need to give him his surprise, to make *me* feel better."

I shake my head. Grace is one of those smart people who seem to have an answer for everything, even things that don't really have one. Normally, people like her really piss me off, because they tend to act like they are so much better than everyone else, even though most of the time, they're full of crap. But even though she says the words, she doesn't act like she *knows*, just that she *believes* it.

And maybe she's right. Or maybe we're both crazy.

As we pull into the park, I go to the same spot I was in last night and turn off my headlights. "Don't get out until I tell you to," I say.

It's dark, but I can see the sparkling river flowing by, and as I get out of the car, I can definitely hear it. "Benny, come out, come out, wherever you are." I scan the riverbank, no Benny, and I'm kind of hoping he took my advice and went over that bridge. I turn around and jump back. He's standing right behind me.

"Damn it, Benny. Don't do that!"

He throws his head back like he's laughing. Great, a ghost with a sense of humor.

"I'm here to make a deal with you," I say.

He rolls his eyes at me.

"Here's the deal. I'll bring Grace to see you, or for you to see her, since she don't believe you're really here. One time. And then, you walk through that grove of trees and do whatever comes next. Deal?"

He looks at me for a long time, like he's thinking.

I laugh. "You're really not in a position to negotiate."

He looks across the water, and so do I, at the grove of trees with the light in the middle. It's a little dimmer than it was last night, and I'm worried that if he doesn't go soon, he won't be able to go at all. I think he thinks the same thing, and he sticks his hand out like he wants to shake on it.

"I'll take your word for it," I say, and I tap on the car window.

Grace is standing next to the car now, looking at me with her head cocked sideways. When Benny sees her, he goes to her side and puts his face down close to her, like he's trying to smell her hair. He tries to touch her, but it just doesn't work that way.

"He's right next to you," I say.

She shuts her eyes and nods. Then she grabs the box from the front seat of the car and walks to a patch of grass and sits on the ground. Benny waves his hand at me like he's trying to shoo me away, which kind of pisses me off. But as long as he leaves when this is over, I'll stay over here by the car. I can still see them, and I kind of want to watch.

"I've been spending time with Jimmy's mom. She is so lost," I hear her say. "They still haven't found him, but I guess you know all that already." She's looking around, talking to air, but I don't want to interrupt her to tell her that he's sitting right in front of her, focusing on her, not her words or the package that lies between them. He looks at her the same way Clay looks at me, and for a minute, I see a different Benny. A doll-collecting, practical joker Benny who loves this woman with all of his soul. Or his energy or whatever. I wish I had known this about him while he was alive.

"Tenesy and your mom are trying to work things out. They really love each other, in a strange way, and well…"

I walk to the bank of the river and decide to throw some rocks. I don't want to be here all night, but I guess if it were the last time I got to talk to Clay, even if I didn't really believe he was there, I'd want a little privacy. Besides, I was hoping she'd spill something juicy, but the conversation is boring as hell.

The light in the trees is getting brighter and is starting to spill toward the river, and I know what that means. It's building the bridge again. Time to wrap this up. I walk back to where Grace is prattling on about something and clear my throat. She stops and looks up at me.

I point at the river. "You better get to your surprise, 'cause I don't think he's going to be here much longer." Benny looks up at me and gives me a pleading look, as if I have any control over it. Then he nods and focuses on Grace.

"Okay. Well, um." She picks up the package and sits it in her lap. "I told you I had a surprise for you, and you said you'd be there no matter what."

He puts both his hands out, palms up, and shrugs.

"And I'm sure you know what's in the box already, but I still need to open it, and…" She looks up at me, and I can tell she feels kind of lost. I nod.

"Okay," she says. She unwraps the gift and opens the box and pulls out a miniature police uniform. It's about the size of one of his porcelain dolls, and I wonder if maybe he plays dress up with them. The uniform is small enough to fit Stormy—

Oh.

The bridge is all the way across the water now, and the colors are indescribable. It's one of the most beautiful things I've ever seen. Someone is walking across, toward our side of the river, and I want to get out of here in case it's Roland.

"It's time to go," I say to Benny, but Grace answers.

"Yes, I guess it is." She stands up, wipes her face, and grabs the baby uniform. "If you can hear me, Benny, I'm going to be okay. I'm going to have a little piece of you, and he's going to be strong, and smart, and wonderful, just like you. Watch over us if you can. I love you, and I'll see you soon."

Grace walks to the car, and I stand there, watching Benny. His head is down, and if a ghost can cry, I think that's what he must be doing.

"Hey, Chief."

I about jump out of my shoes and turn to see Jimmy Ray Wiley, smiling, holding a Chihuahua. I glance quickly at Grace in the car. She has her head lowered, then I remember she can't see him anyway. Benny stands and nods to me then looks toward the car and makes the little hand sign again. Two fingers to the chest then pointing toward his eyes. Then he turns to Jimmy and smiles, and together they walk toward the bridge.

I watch them walk across the water. It's hard to look away from the light, and when they are about halfway across, it explodes in color, brighter than any fireworks display I've ever seen, and is swept back into the grove of trees.

Grace is out of the car, moving quickly toward me. "What was that?"

"You saw that?" I ask.

"I don't know what I saw. A flash of light?" She looks a little scared and a little hopeful, and all I can do is smile.

"It was him, wasn't it?" Grace and I both turn when we hear another voice, and Tina Early is standing beside the rest area, looking at us.

None of us move or speak.

Things just got a whole lot more complicated.

Chapter 28
Tina

Harley is right. I may need to talk to someone. A professional. I think I'm losing my mind.

After we got home from the funeral, I wanted to curl up on the couch and crawl inside my own head. But something Dr. Phil said this week keeps playing in my mind: "We all make our choices, and, good or bad, we deal with the consequences." I think he was talking about me, or to me, and now I know why people can't turn off his show.

At the funeral, Grace's words to me meant a lot. Benny and I were friends, and I don't have a lot of those. She was kind and hugged me sincerely then went about the business of burying her husband. She will never know the truth about what happened that day, at least if I have anything to say about it, but even if she did, I think she'd understand. Benny chose Maryanne over himself. I was just his tool in making that happen. If I allow myself to believe that, I can get through this too.

So I went about my afternoon straightening up the house, and when the boys got home from their grandmother's, I even spent the evening listening to them tell of their adventures from the past week. But I was feeling antsy, as if I still needed to resolve something, and it wasn't going to happen here.

I told Harley I was going for a drive, and I was glad it was already dark outside, because I didn't want to see any more of the loss still evident in Deacon. I knew it was still there, but the darkness hid it. As

I crossed the bridge at Beecher Creek, I looked up and saw the cross, still lit on the side of the hill, a week later. I slowly drove through the park, the area of grass where Clay landed, the spot where Benny died, and parked my Hummer on the other side of the building that housed the public restrooms. No one from the road could see my truck there, and I wanted to be alone.

The creek was back to its lazy drift. The water was dark and peaceful. I closed my eyes and cracked my window so I could hear the water in the distance.

Then I heard a car door slam, and as my eyes shot open, I briefly saw the headlights on the water before they were shut off. I thought it must be some teenagers sneaking down to the river for some make-out time and had my hand on the key, ready to fire up the engine, when I heard Cass Adams's voice, and it chilled me to the bone.

She was calling Benny's name.

Angus had told me once—in confidence, of course—that Cass went to the Hill to talk to Roland after he first passed. That wasn't a big surprise, as I think a lot of people tend to do the same thing. The difference was, Angus said she thinks he talks back to her, that she actually sees him. And that's delusional. I know she's had problems her entire life, and it made me feel sorry for her, but maybe it made her feel better about everything? God knows I'd like to say a few words to Benny right now and *believe* that he hears me.

She began talking, and her side of the conversation was so believable, I could almost picture him standing there. Then another car door. Then Grace.

Oh no. I quietly got out of the Hummer and moved to the back of the public building. I wanted to stop this, wanted to protect Grace, somehow, from being sucked into Cass Adams's delusion. But I couldn't move beyond my hidden spot, entranced by the scene I was witnessing. Aside from the fact that Benny was nowhere to be seen, *it was so real*.

Grace got back in the car, and yet I still couldn't move. Cass was staring at the river, and I couldn't help but look that way too.

Then came a bright flash of light, a burst of color over the river that shot through the grove of trees on the other side. I've never seen anything so beautiful, so ethereal, in my entire life, and I expect I never will.

Oh. My. God.

As Grace got out of the car, I was propelled from my hiding spot and moved slowly from behind the building.

"It was him, wasn't it?"

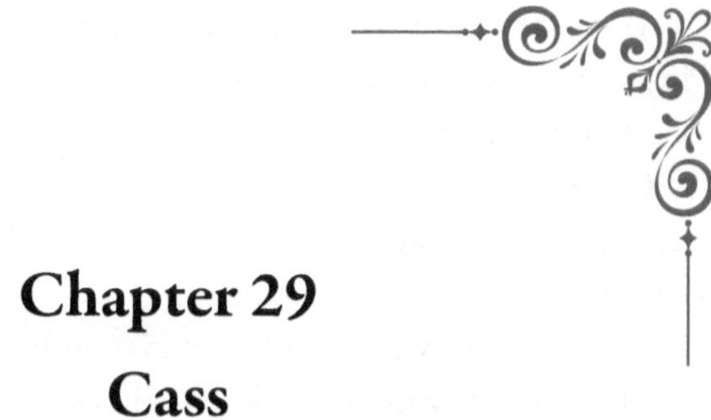

Chapter 29
Cass

"Tina?" Grace says. And I'm glad she does, because that means she can see her, too, and that means she isn't dead. But it also means Tina just saw everything that happened, and although I got up the courage to let Grace in on my secret, now there are two who will know, and that can't be good.

She's moving toward us like she's punch-drunk, and she keeps looking at the water. "The light," she says. "I saw it." She wraps her arms around Grace, and the two stand there, holding each other, looking at me, then at the water, then back at me.

I want to run and hide under the nearest rock I can find. I know people like Tina and Grace want explanations, and I figured with just Grace, I could get away with "Sure, it's just energy," and Benny would go away, and Grace wouldn't say much. But now I have no explanations. I don't even know how to explain it to myself.

"Grams says it's my gift," I say softly, but I'm looking at the ground. I can't look at them. I don't do vulnerable very well, but here I am, and it gives me a pain in my chest, and I—

"It must be difficult."

I lift my head, and Grace is looking at me in the same way I looked at Dog the first time Clay brought him home. Tina slowly nods.

Then they both walk toward me, and I back up a little at first, but Tina wraps her arms around me, and so does Grace, and they hold me until I quit shaking.

Grace takes a deep breath. "I have reincarnation dreams almost every night. They are so real, I wake up and don't know where I am sometimes."

"I don't know what that is, but it sounds scary as hell," Tina says.

"They are. Benny didn't know. Babe Shatner is the only one that knows."

"Grams?" I say.

Grace smiles. "Yes. She's been trying to help me understand."

"Yeah, Grams is good at that." She's good at a lot of things.

"It isn't really a gift, though," she says.

"To be honest, Grace, I'll take any dirt I can get on you to keep you from telling anyone about tonight," I say. And I intend to get some on Tina, even if we are girl-bonding in a weird way.

"Money," Tina finally says. "That's my gift. Since I was just a kid, I knew how to take a nickel and make it a dollar. I know it doesn't sound like a bad thing, but it's like I have to do it, all the time, and sometimes, I'm afraid what would happen if I fail. So it's all I do, and my kids don't see me much."

I pull back and smile a little. The fact that Tina can make money out of rocks is no secret, but I know what she's trying to do, and another feeling runs through me that I'm not used to having—compassion.

"That's it?" Grace asks with a nervous laugh.

"Oh, we're talking secrets," Tina says. She lowers herself slowly to the ground and pats the grass beside her. "I have eight cats. And my husband thinks he was abducted by aliens."

Grace looks at me and smiles, and for the first time in my life, I don't feel so alone. So foreign. So... different.

Chapter 30
Tina

J ust one more dab of paint.

"Hurry up, Tina. It ain't much of an open house if we don't actually open the doors," Harley says.

I stand back and admire my hand-stenciled words on the wall:

Make a Choice.

Take a Chance.

Change Your World.

Grace puts an arm around me. I can tell it's her without even looking. She always smells like honeysuckle. Fresh. Clean. "It's perfect," she says. "Where's Cass?"

"I'm coming." She's wearing an oversized flannel shirt, rolled up at the sleeves, and it's long enough to be a dress. Her hair is tucked up in a baseball cap, and her face and hands have more paint on them than the walls. *That's Cass.* She looks at my wall then scrunches her face together. "It looks good, but you spelled 'your' wrong."

"What?" I turn quickly with my paintbrush in hand.

Grace laughs. "Stop it, Cass. She's nervous enough as it is."

"I couldn't help it. Chill out, Tina. It's great. Everything is great," she says.

It's been three months since that night that Grace, Cass, and I sat in the park by Beecher Creek and formed a bond like I've never had with other women before. All this time, we were right there, within reach of each other, and too scared, or too selfish, or too wrapped up in our own worlds to just reach out and find each other. We laughed, we cried, we told each other our secrets. Not all of them, of course. Grace will never know the truth about the day Benny died. And we all realized something: we're all damaged, we're all flawed, and we're all special.

"Okay. Let's do this." I turn to my left and nod to Angus, who is standing in the doorway of the adjoining room. Sammie and Sonja have their hands full of pamphlets to give out to the people coming to see my new business, Inspirations. Angus nods back. "Okay, Harley, we're all ready."

"We better go," Grace says.

"No, I want you here, both of you."

"I need to take a bath in turpentine," Cass says. "I'll clean up, get Stormy, and be back in a few hours."

"And I'll be back after I pick up Josie," Grace says. Josie, Benny's mother, moved in with Grace about two months ago after Tenesy got sent back to prison. He was in town long enough to bury his son then beat Rudy Drown almost to death in his sleep. He was dumb enough to videotape the entire thing and put it on the internet. I doubt he'll ever get out now. Rudy resigned as sheriff and left town. He said it was time for him to retire, but I think he was just so humiliated by the video, he couldn't take it. That'll teach him to sleep in the nude. Darnell Dix easily won in an emergency election. He's an okay guy, and I think he'll serve the county well.

Jerri Lynn Harper, followed by Daze, is the first one through the door. But no sign of Beth. Figures.

"I'm definitely out of here," Cass says. I give her a hug and watch as she goes out the back way. Grace squeezes my arm and follows her.

I turn to my first official member: Jerri Lynn Harper. "Congratulations, young lady. As the first person through that door, you get a free membership for a year," I say.

"Sweet," she says.

Daze shakes his head. "Not until I know exactly what that means. She's only sixteen."

"Which means she can take advantage of everything here, except Angus's tattoo shop. She'd need parental authorization for that."

"And she ain't getting it," he says, looking at her.

"So, what exactly do you do in here, Tina?" Daze asks.

"This main building is where we hold classes and have events," I say to Jerri as I open the pamphlet she's holding and point at the next month's schedule. "It changes every month, but the self-defense classes and yoga will definitely be ongoing."

Daze looks over her shoulder and shakes his head. "Book signings, candle parties, Lamaze classes. Sounds like a bunch of women's stuff to me."

After the tornado, I thought about what I really wanted to do. I've been serving men in this town for so long, I thought it was time I did something for everyone. Angus and I bought three attached buildings downtown that hadn't been destroyed and revitalized them. Little Bit of Ink II is housed in one building; the other two are mine to run.

"Men are always welcome," I say. "Go next door and see the gym. There's a sauna in there, and a massage room."

"Fat Tina has a gym," Daze snickers.

I turn to him and smile. "*Tina* has a gym. A gym without judgment. If you go in there, you leave your negativity outside."

Jerri laughs. "She told you."

"This looks real nice, Tina," Harvey Cox says as he finds his way through the crowd. And there is a crowd, people not only from Deacon, but I notice some from Columbia and Springtown.

I can't help but glance at Harvey's crotch. Of course Cass told us. Some secrets are just too good to keep. "Thanks, Harvey. The uniform looks good on you."

After Benny died, the mayor named Harvey as the new chief. He's young but experienced, and he cares about the community. He was a good choice.

"Big boots to fill," he says. He was also a good friend of Benny's, and I know he misses him as much as I do.

The radio on his belt squawks, and Levi Dinger's voice comes through. "Chief, I just got a call from Bobby Leo. He said Billy Jack is passed out in his cornfield and looks like he's wet himself."

Chief. It's going to take a while for me to get used to that.

"On my way, Levi." Harvey looks at me and shrugs. Before he leaves, he takes one more look around. "A lot of guys around here are going to miss the club, but this is a good business for the community. You may not make as much money at this place."

I smile and nod. "Oh, I don't know about that."

You see, I have this gift.

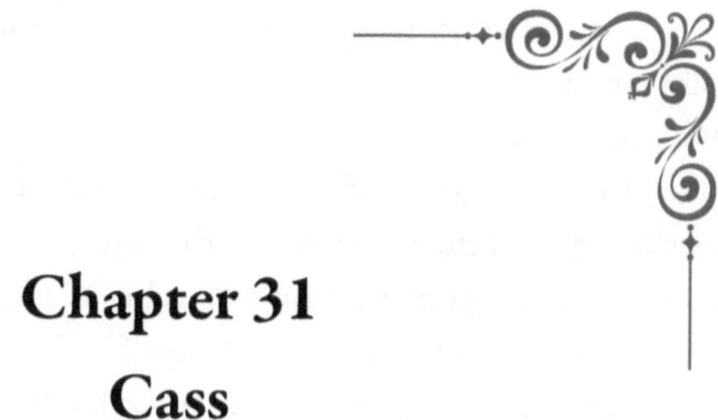

Chapter 31

Cass

Stormy, Dog, and I are lying on our stomachs on a blanket in the backyard, playing our most recent favorite game of "lift your head up off the ground." Stormy pushes up with her arms and holds her head up and looks around for a few seconds then lays it back down and giggles. She's getting better at it. She doesn't look as much like a bobblehead as she did when she first started trying, and I think I'm getting better at it too. Dog has it down pat.

Clay's brother Britt and his boyfriend, Dennis, have been up several times over the summer to check on me and Clay. I think they just wanted another excuse to come see Stormy. I can't blame them for that. They said they're going to spoil her rotten, and true to their word, they had a castle delivered that Angus, Clay, and Harlan Early are trying to put together next to the new worm huts.

"I think the castle part goes on the left," Clay says. Britt and Dennis have been wanting to buy Stormy a swing set to put in the backyard since the day she was born. We told them she was too young, but finally, once the house was finished, Clay gave in and said okay, might as well put it up this weekend. We didn't know they were talking about a deluxe cedar one, complete with a rock climbing wall, sand pit, wavy slide, and castle.

"If another tornado comes, we'll just hide in your castle," I say. Stormy lifts her head up, turns to me, then starts giggling again. She likes to laugh.

"The castle goes in the middle," Harlan says. "The regular swings go to the left, and the tire swing to the right, then the picnic table." Three men, putting together a swing set as big as a house, and all too good for the directions. Figures.

Stormy and Dog are talking to each other like they do. He makes little sounds to her, and she babbles back. I listen, trying to understand their conversation, but it's between them. I'm hoping her first word will be "Momma," but I have a feeling it's going to be "Dog." I expect he'll teach her to bark first, anyway.

"Stormy wants to know where she's supposed to tie up her pony," I say.

"A pony! What a great idea!" Angus says. "She can keep it at my house."

"No ponies. At least for a few years." That's Clay, putting his foot down.

I lean down and whisper to Stormy, "Start thinking of a name for it now." She lifts her head up and looks at me and smiles. I stick my tongue out, and she does the same.

"Break time," Clay says. He kneels down and kisses me on the forehead then picks Stormy up and lifts her way above his head. She squeals and kicks her hands and feet. She loves her daddy, and Clay is the proudest man in town. He's had a rough time with the physical therapy, still has a lot of pain at times, and walks with a limp. But he doesn't complain.

Angus goes for drinks, and Harlan sits with us on our blanket. It's a beautiful day—the sun is out, but it's not too hot, and a slight breeze is blowing to remind us that fall is coming fast. "Where's Tina?" I ask Harlan. "She was supposed to be here thirty minutes ago."

"She said she had to check on the gym on her way out. You know how she is," he says.

Yes, I do, and getting to know how she is more each day. It's still strange to me, having friends, and even stranger that I know so much about them. The real them. I had Maryanne, but I think the reason she and I got along at all was that we were both damaged, and for some reason, I thought we were the only ones. It was as if everyone else, women like Tina and Grace, for instance, had everything they needed and were always happy, and that made me not like them. But the truth is, we all have problems; some just hide them better than others. And Tina is a lot funnier than Maryanne was. Grace is a lot nicer. And neither one of them call me crazy—they call me Cass, and I like that.

Grace and Grams come out of the house with Angus, carrying glasses and a bottle of juice for the baby. "You guys haven't got that thing built yet?" Grace asks.

Angus takes a long drink and wipes his mouth with the back of his hand. "No. Maybe if you ladies could chip in and help, we'd get it done a little faster." He smiles that million-dollar smile, and I notice how much he likes to tease Grace. After Grace lost Benny and Angus broke up with Maryanne, they've become good friends. I know they aren't romantically involved, it's only been three months, but in my eyes, she could do a lot worse than a guy like him. And when you lose someone you love, it's nice to have someone else who can sympathize with you. Of course, I lost my husband a little over a year ago, but I don't think it counts if you killed him.

Grace rubs her belly bump. "Sorry, can't help you guys. I'm pregnant."

Grams shakes her head. "Not me, I'm old."

They all look at me. "Not me either. I'm... just not going to help."

"I'll help," Shaylene says as she bounces out the door while holding a brown cardboard box. She looks so much like her mother at that age that sometimes I have to remind myself that those days are long past.

Maryanne left a month ago. Said she had a job lined up in San Diego and was moving to the West Coast to start over. I hope she finds what she's looking for.

"But," Shaylene adds, looking at Angus, "only if I get to keep a sweet find I made at your place this morning." Angus's house is almost done, and Shaylene has taken it upon herself to plant a bunch of flowers around to make it look more homey. I remember someone else who used to do that. I shake the memory of Roland and his rosebushes from my head.

Angus holds his hands up in defense. "I take no responsibility for anything you dig up out there."

"This is classic. The face is cracked, but I think that makes it look even weirder. It looks just like the one Dad used to have in the kitchen. I'd love to clean it up and hang it in my dorm room." I look up, and Shaylene is holding Roland's damn black cat clock. The one whose eyes used to watch everything I did, the one whose screech used to send me over the edge every hour. I'm going to have to learn to bury things a little deeper.

Clay looks at me, and I shrug. *Hey, I tried.* At least she didn't dig up a body out there.

I think Angus realizes by my and Clay's reactions that there may be a story behind the stupid clock. "I think that belongs to—"

"It's fine," Clay says. "It was your grandma's. She'd like it that someone has it who actually thinks it's 'sweet.'"

Some things you just never seem to get rid of. But if it's hanging on a dorm room wall halfway across the state, at least it isn't staring at us every day.

Clay hands Stormy to Grams, and she gives her the bottle while they all go back to work. Grams is singing to her, some Jim Morrison song about telling your name and I love you, or something like that. Stormy listens to every word and slowly closes her eyes in Grams's arms.

"See, she likes the Doors, just like her old Grams." Grams lays her down on the blanket, and she, Grace, and I walk over to watch the progress on the swing set. Dog stays with Stormy, laying his head down next to her and shutting his eyes too.

"We should have this done about the time Grace gives birth," Harlan says.

"Well, Stormy's going to need a friend to help her break it in, anyway," Clay says. "Every princess needs a knight to guard her castle."

"Or another princess," Grace says.

Dog starts barking, and Stormy is giggling, and we all turn to see that she's lying on her back, pedaling her feet and swinging her arms. "She turned over!" Clay says. He drops his tools and is next to her on the blanket, holding her hand in his.

"She's so proud of herself," Grams says, "and look, Dog is jumping in the air like he's saying he's proud too."

I just stand there. Oh, I'm looking, all right. And I know what she's giggling about. "It's okay, Dog," I say, and he looks at me, jumps up in front of Stormy one more time, then runs to me and whines. I scratch the back of his head. Angus, Harley, and Shaylene continue to work, while Grams and Grace join Clay on the blanket. I lean down to Dog and whisper. "It's okay, Dog. That's her grandma tickling her feet with a flower. But nobody else sees her but you and me, so shhhh."

Dog looks at me and cocks his head, and I let out a long sigh.

"Yeah, I know. Stormy sees her too."

Acknowledgements

Cass Adams and I have been on quite a journey over the past several years, but we haven't been alone. Thank you to my readers, who make my crazy world a little brighter every day.

My list of people to thank is long, so bear with me:

My family—Joe, Dillon, Theron, Kerry, Anthony, Milam, and Brittan. Eighty percent of the time, I'm pretty awesome. I'm glad you all stick around for the other twenty.

Angela McRae, my editor for *Call Me Cass*, and everyone at Red Adept. You have made this entire publishing experience a pleasure. Thanks for taking me on and being there every step of the way.

Kelley Hartmann McDowell for showing me baby goat pictures when I needed them, and even naming one after me.

Chance X Sledge, Body Piercer Extraordinaire, for our late-night discussion of genital body piercing, which wasn't creepy at all. You, sir, are an artist and a gentleman.

Carrie Rago for reading my stories all through junior high and high school and thinking they were funny.

Allan Dinger and James McDowell for teaching me everything I ever wanted to know about turkey hunting even though that scene never made the book.

Jim Clark, for getting my book in the hands of the Eli Young Band. How about Nancy Sinatra next?

David Harper and Taco the Chihuahua, just for being David and Taco.

Laura Cox, why won't you age like the rest of us?

Troy, the best bartender ever.

My editor and friend Rebecca Mahoney for telling me to rewrite this book at least three times before it ever made it to Red Adept. You were right, as usual.

Kendra Gross and everyone at Southeastern Oklahoma State University for a job I love, coworkers and students who keep me thinking, and a drama-free workplace.

Linda Potts, Dana Lane, and all the librarians at the Idabel Public Library for being so supportive of my work.

Rick, Craig, Merle, and Bob. Once on the team, always on the team.

Suzi Spencer, Stacey Roberts, Beth Garland, and David Rawding for loving my work and telling everybody!

And to Robert Saugus (Bobby Sox) and all the other pirates: keep writing, keep exploring, keep inspiring. And don't forget the mixers.

About the Author

Kelly Stone Gamble was born and raised in a small Midwestern town but, as an adult, became a city girl. As a member of the faculty at Southeastern Oklahoma State University, she now moves between her homes in Henderson, Nevada, and Idabel, Oklahoma, allowing her to enjoy the best of both worlds.

Read more at www.kstonegamble.com.

About the Publisher

Dear Reader,

We hope you enjoyed this book. Please consider leaving a review on your favorite book site.

Visit https://RedAdeptPublishing.com to see our entire catalogue.

Don't forget to subscribe to our monthly newsletter to be notified of future releases and special sales.